Mommy! I have to go Potty!

A Parent's Guide to Toilet Training

By Jan Faull, M.Ed.

R&R

Raefield-Roberts,
Roberts,
Publishers

Acknowledgments

Thanks to: my family who playfully displayed interest in this book's topic; my colleagues, who provided ideas and feedback; my network of telephone friends, who broke up the solitude of writing; all the parents who offered stories and details for this book; and to Debbie, who taught me to write.

In memory of Elena Hovander

ISBN 0-9650477-0-9
LC 96-68504

Cover design and illustration by
Rebekah Strecker, copyright © 1996

Co-Published by:
Raefield-Roberts, Publishers
10214 183rd Ave E
Bonney Lake, WA 98390

and

Parenting Press, Inc.
P.O. Box 75267
Seattle, WA 98175

CONTENTS

INTRODUCTION

$\int$uccessful toilet training—that is, training completed with as little emotional upheaval as possible, in a time frame attuned to the child—requires a blend of techniques on the part of the parent, and readiness and willingness on the part of the child.

This book will show you how to familiarize your child with using the toilet so that when his body develops to the point where he's able to hold in his urine and stool and release it at will, he'll be interested and willing to use this new ability.

Each child who learns to use the toilet does so in a unique way. Every mother, father, childcare provider, or grandparent who has ever trained a child has advice for everyone else on how to proceed.

This book is written for today's parents. This is a broad-based group and many differences in toilet training approaches exist. There are differences from one generation to the next. Within any one family there are techniques that worked with one child but needed altering for the second.

Most children are successfully trained by the age of three and a half. For some it occurs easily, for others many accidents and power plays between parent and child occur along the way. Each child has his own time frame for training. The parent's job is to determine when his readiness alarm clock goes off and guide him to toileting success. For some children it's an alarm clock bell, loud and clear; you know exactly when they're ready. For others it's more like a snooze alarm—the child wakes up to the idea of learning to use the toilet, but keeps drifting back to sleep and needs waking up again and again.

No matter how you approach guiding your child to use the toilet, there are four points to keep in mind before you get started.

First, toilet training involves the most personal part of a child's body. Anyone training a child needs to show respect for the child's most private parts and proceed in a dignified manner.

Second, urinating and having a bowel movement are natural and necessary parts of everyone's day. We all eat, sleep, and eliminate. We want children to have pleasant associations with this natural process. If parents yell, spank, express frustration, or act disgusted, children may develop negative associations with toileting. So keep your demeanor and attitude positive during the toilet training process.

Third, cultivate your child's interest in using the toilet. If your child senses this activity is mostly for your benefit, she might balk. Don't make toilet training more important to you than it is to your child. If you're doubtful about how to proceed, it's best to do less rather than more. Always remember that ultimate control lies with your child.

Fourth, as you proceed with toilet training, don't let the process dominate your relationship. Yes it's important, but you still need to read stories, play, and talk with your child about topics unrelated to toileting.

So, read on. Gather ideas, keep in mind your child's uniqueness, and develop a plan that works for you both.

Jan Faull
The Potty Coach

1

GETTING TOTALLY READY FOR TRAINING

Toilet training is not an isolated event of simply learning to urinate and have bowel movements in the toilet. The process involves four aspects of your developing child: physical, intellectual, social, and emotional. It's important to understand how each of these areas contributes to teaching a child to use the toilet.

Before taking a look at your child however, it's important to define your role. Picture a basketball game. Your child is the player. Most of the time the parent's role is that of cheerleader. As a member of the cheer squad you're thrilled and enthusiastic with each step he takes toward victory. If your child has a few accidents or even regresses temporarily, you don't get discouraged; you know that, sooner or later, success will happen. Even if he appears to be down by twenty points in the potty training process, any slight advancement gets applause. As "toileting cheerleader," you don't necessarily need pom pons and a "sis boom bah." What your child needs most from you is positive attention for any interest he shows or slight advances he makes in toileting skills.

Sometimes a parent's role is that of coach. There are times when you need to step in, teach some skills, and coach your child to toileting success. And all good coaches recognize the importance of practice, practice, practice. The parent-as-coach needs to sense when the time is right to nudge the player into learning the next skill and gaining more competency.

There are also times when a parent needs to referee; it's up to you to establish some rules and guidelines for potty training.

Most of the time, though, you are a cheerleader. Just as a cheer squad never gets down on the team, you never get down on your child. When ultimate success occurs, you're relieved and thrilled. A developmental milestone has been reached. However, it's important to remember that this is the child's achievement and victory, not yours.

PHYSICAL READINESS

Now that your role is defined, it's time to look at your child from the four different aspects of toilet training readiness. The first is physical.

Children can't walk until their muscles are developed enough to carry them across the room. They can't write the alphabet until their fine finger muscles are ready to form intricate shapes. A child can't be potty trained until the bowel and bladder muscles are strong.

In order to be toilet trained, these muscles must be developed sufficiently to hold in the urine and stool. For infants and toddlers, pee and poop* simply come out when the bladder or bowel is full. When a child is physically ready to be toilet trained, the muscles are strong enough to keep in the urine and stool and then release them when the child decides the time is right.

Notice if your child's diaper is dry for an hour and a half or so. This is your first indication that the bladder muscles are developing. If your child is constantly wet, he simply isn't ready.

As your child plays, notice if he stops his activity when he's having a bowel movement. If he does, it is a sign he knows something is happening with his body. Comment, "You're pooping in your diaper. Someday you'll go in the toilet." He isn't ready to use the toilet, but it's significant that he recognizes what he's doing. If your child actually gets up and walks to his bedroom to have a bowel movement in his diaper, he has developed control of his rectal muscles.

Stories from the Bathroom

❱ Nathan was two and a half and Mom was ready to start educating him to use the toilet. He was willing to sit on the toilet, but never performed. So Mom and Nathan shopped for special superhero underwear. Nathan was excited to wear these underpants. For three days Mom tried training Nathan. He wet his pants hourly. Pee would run down his leg but Nathan would not feel a thing. He just kept playing.

---

*In this book you'll see the words "pee" and "poop" used throughout because they are the potty training words most used and easily recognized by children. Some families use the words "wet" and "messy." Use whatever toileting vocabulary is comfortable for you and understandable to the child's caregivers.

It was clear Nathan had no internal messages about "the need to go." Mom put him back in diapers, but because Nathan insisted on wearing the superhero underpants, she just stretched them over his diapers and waited until his body developed further.

When you look for signs of physical readiness, it's important to note if your child is over the thrill of learning to walk and run. The sturdy walker and confident runner who now sits on the floor to play with toys will be more willing to sit on the toilet than the child who still wants to practice running.

SOCIAL READINESS

Your next step is to recognize that steering children toward toileting is easier if they participate in it as a social experience. The question for most parents is, how in the world do you make toileting social? Try the following ideas.

First, take your child with you to use the toilet and encourage him to do the flushing. Put a potty chair in the bathroom and when you use the toilet, encourage him to sit on the little potty chair. In the beginning, don't bother taking his diapers off and don't expect any success. Just get him accustomed to sitting on the potty. Talk and enjoy this time together. Be encouraging and say, "Someday you'll use the toilet just like Mom or Dad."

Some children won't want a little toilet on the floor, they'll want to sit on the big toilet. If this is the case with your child, purchase a potty seat that fits on the big toilet.

Encourage your child to set dolls and Teddy bears on the potty seat to play toileting. Through play children learn about toileting. If Teddy accidentally falls in the toilet, calmly rescue him and allow the play to continue. Your child will learn from this experience that if he falls in, like

Teddy, he will be rescued and not flushed away. All of these activities help children warm up to the idea of using the toilet themselves.

Traditionally, moms are the most involved in teaching toileting techniques, so girls often train more quickly than boys. Girls have bodies like mom, they see what she does, and they learn from modeling after her behavior. When dads get involved in training boys, it helps them succeed. If the same-sex parent isn't involved, a child will still learn to use the toilet, it may just take a little longer.

It really helps if your child can watch another child who is similar in age perform on the toilet. This puts the toileting process in his realm of possibility. He thinks: If my cousin can do it, so can I. If there are older brothers and sisters in the house, encourage the younger child to watch them in the bathroom (but only with permission from the older child). Remember, children together in the bathroom always need adult supervision.

Modeling by peers is often all it takes for toileting success to occur. For children in a child care setting, social readiness is naturally encouraged since children want to participate in the bathroom activities along with the others.

Stories from the Bathroom

❧ John at four was urine-trained but determined not to poop in the toilet. Each night after his bedtime story, John pooped in his diaper and called Mom to clean him up. Then one day when friend Jeremy came to play, John watched him have a bowel movement in the toilet. John was impressed with Jeremy's ability and skill. He decided that if Jeremy, who was his same age and size, could poop in the toilet, so could he. Now John has his bowel movement at bedtime, in the toilet, before his story.

Another sign of social readiness is imitation. Does your child mimic you shaving, cooking or shopping? If so, he may be ready to imitate toileting practices too. This is a good sign.

INTELLECTUAL READINESS

A positive social bathroom experience increases readiness, but your child also needs to make the connection between his mind and body about "the need to go." This is intellectual readiness. Some verbal ability to communicate about the process of peeing and pooping is also necessary. They need words—a toileting vocabulary. It's best to use words, such as pee, poop, urinate and bowel movement, that are understandable not only to people in your home, but to teachers, nurses, child care providers, and other parents too. Cutesy terms—si-si and ka-ka—familiar only in your household won't help your child when she ventures beyond the boundaries of your home.

For your child, intellectual readiness comes in three steps. The first is awareness that she "has gone." The day she indicates with words or body language that her diapers are full or wet and need changing is an important first step.

The next step is awareness from your child that she "is going" right now. Comments like, "Poop is coming out, Mom" or, "I feel the pee dripping down my leg" show that she has reached the second step. The child in underpants who never notices poop or wetness is not ready; put the diapers back on for a few months.

The realization of "is going" is important, but it's the last step that indicates a child is close to being trained: the knowledge of "needing to go." When your daughter comes to you and says, "Dad, I need to pee," get up and put her on the toilet immediately. She has made a connection between her mind and body; she can hold the urine in until she is on the toilet and then release it.

Watch for the time when your child is almost obsessive about knowing where shoes, coats, purses, grocery bags, and pajamas belong. Since she now knows that certain items belong in special places, she'll also understand better that pee and poop go in the toilet.

EMOTIONAL READINESS

Some children sneak off to their bedroom to poop in their diapers. This tells parents the child is ready intellectually because she understands the "need to go," but may not be ready to give up her diapers. She lacks emotional readiness. It's okay, all she needs is time and reassurance that she's the one in control. She, and she alone, will decide when the time is right to use the toilet.

It's a myth that all children want to give up wet and messy diapers. Wearing diapers is all they've known since birth, and it feels normal. Change only rarely comes easily to children.

Peeing and pooping in the toilet can be scary. Some children fear they'll fall in and be flushed away. Other children don't like their poop (part of their bodies) falling out of them, into the toilet and disappearing.[**]

If children appear fearful and reluctant, pushing does no good. If your son states clearly, "No, I don't like the toilet," no amount of coaxing and persuading is going to change his mind. Do not engage in a power struggle. It's best to back off and try another approach later. Emotional power struggles over toileting (a battle of wills between parent and child) are counter productive to toilet training.

[**]The book *Toilet Learning* by Alison Mack includes a section for children about where their poop and pee go when flushed. See the Suggested Reading List at the end of this book.

Guiding your child to use the toilet usually takes place between the ages of two and three, when a child is pushing hard to be independent and is frequently negative. This adds to the challenge of training. As parents, there's a lot you can do to influence your child's behavior, but your control only goes so far. Ultimately, it is the child who decides to be trained—*he* is in control of his body. Instructing your children to use the toilet really shows you where your influence begins and ends.

One way to promote emotional readiness is to start taking your child to sit on his potty seat twice a day, beginning at about age two. Do this at two scheduled times—perhaps after breakfast and before bed. The child can be fully clothed. Starting this routine at age two, before your child is totally ready to be trained, gets him in the habit of using the toilet. Whether he performs or not is unimportant. Working this practice time into the daily schedule helps the child make the transition from using diapers to using the toilet. If you use this approach, chances are better that when your child is physically ready, he will be emotionally ready too. Going to the toilet will not be a foreign experience as it's part of the daily routine. Many children have a natural interest in toileting. For them, imposing a potty practice time is not necessary.

To become emotionally ready, a child needs acceptance of his fears, and reassurance that Mom and Dad respect the fact that it's his body and ultimate control lies with him.

Social, intellectual, and physical readiness are often easier to detect than emotional readiness. If your child is not mature enough to give up wearing diapers or if he's feeling pressure to train and resists, it's usually a sign he is not emotionally ready. So back off and try again in a couple of months. A child who is emotionally ready is eager and interested to try to use the toilet.

Stories from the Bathroom

❧ A week before Alan turned three he was reluctant and unwilling to potty train. He didn't like that little potty chair on the floor and he wouldn't sit on the plastic ring that fit on the big toilet either. It wobbled.

Alan was ready physically, intellectually, and socially, but emotionally he wasn't quite there. Finally one day he agreed to sit on the big toilet, but he wanted to do it without the plastic ring.

Mom and Dad were encouraged. So Alan sat on the toilet, teetering back and forth, trying to get his balance. Then, he slipped. His little bottom dropped into the toilet. Not only did the fall frighten him, but he was terrified of being flushed away. He yelled, "Don't flush the toilet, don't flush the toilet!" Mom pulled him out, held him, and affirmed how scary it was for him. After that, of course, Alan was more determined than ever not to use the toilet. Days passed. Mom kept asking him if he'd like to try. All she got were flat-out refusals.

Finally Dad took the initiative. He said, "Come on Alan, let's try again. I'll hold you on the toilet so you won't fall." Alan resisted, but Dad confidently set him on the toilet anyway. Dad crouched around the toilet, encircling Alan with his arms. Dad reassured him, "I'm here, I won't let you fall in, you're safe. Go ahead, you can pee in the toilet just like Dad." Alan didn't pee but his fears began to disappear. Each evening Dad included taking Alan to the toilet as part of the bedtime routine. After three days of following this routine, Alan finally did urinate in the toilet.

Dad sensed Alan needed emotional support to help him on the road to toilet training. All it took was some reassurance and understanding.

Dad also knew the hard-line approach: "Get in there right now and pee in that toilet. You're not afraid of a dumb old toilet, are you? What are you, a baby?"—would probably result in a power struggle and emotional damage to his son.

So this was the beginning for Alan. He was getting over his fear of the toilet, and emotionally he was on his way to being trained. For a week or so Mom and Dad held him safely in place as he peed and pooped. Finally Alan felt confident enough to balance alone on the toilet without assistance. In less than three weeks he was totally trained.

READINESS CHECKLIST

Here are questions to ask yourself when considering your child's readiness:

☑ Is your child's diaper dry for at least an hour and a half at a time?

☑ Does your child stop playing when he's pushing a poop into his diaper?

☑ Is your child over the fascination of learning to walk and run? Does she enjoy sitting and playing with toys?

☑ Does your child mention or indicate that his diapers are wet or full, or that he has just peed or pooped?

☑ Does your child know when she is in the process of peeing or pooping?

☑ Does your child indicate "the need to go?"

☑ Does your child like to put shoes, coats, and books where they belong?

☑ Does your child imitate your behavior: cooking, shaving, shopping?

☑ Does your child put dolls or stuffed animals on the toilet? Does he follow you and others into the bathroom to watch you pee or poop? Does he like being part of the bathroom social scene?

☑ Is your child comfortable and not afraid of sitting on the toilet?

☑ Is your child willing to sit on the toilet twice a day as part of the daily routine?

If you answered "yes" to most of these eleven questions, your child is ready for toileting instruction.

As your child matures physically, intellectually, socially, and emotionally, your role is not to sit back as a silent observer. There's a lot you can subtly do to help the process along. But since your approach is most likely going to be different from your child's Grandma's, you need to understand how her generation approached toilet training.

2

IN GRANDMA'S DAY

"Your child isn't toilet trained yet? All my children were trained by eighteen months. You'd better get that child trained or he'll be wetting his pants in kindergarten."

Parents today must prepare themselves for an avalanche of unsolicited advice from Grandma, Aunt Louise, and Betty next door. Anyone who ever trained a child has advice and opinions. And it's true, yesterday's parents started earlier, took charge of the toilet training process, and were determined to train as soon and as quickly as possible.

How Grandma claims her children were completely trained at eighteen months or sooner is a mystery today. But it's clear that directing children to use the toilet in the last generation was definitely a result of the mother's interest and determination, not the child's. Toileting instruction was incorporated into daily living; Mother was disciplined to take her child to the toilet on a regular basis.

TOILETING COMPETITION

Early training success provided an avenue for bragging: The sooner your child trained, the more accomplished your parenting. In some circles parents even linked early toilet learning to a child's intelligence. Aunt Helen labeled her youngest daughter the smartest because at sixteen months, she peed in the toilet on command. Today, we know there's little connection between early toilet training and a child's IQ.

This is how Jackie (mother of three adult daughters and now grandmother of two) describes teaching her children to use the toilet.

Stories from the Bathroom

❥ Laundry was so much work that you wanted to get your children trained as soon as possible. I had a washer but no dryer. All the mothers in the neighborhood hung laundry out to dry. Living in the midwest, this was hard work all year round.

Your skill as a parent was measured by how early your children trained. Everyone in the neighborhood noticed the day you hung training pants out to dry—diapers no longer there. It was a proud moment. Competition raged in the neighborhood for whose child trained youngest.

I started my girls around fourteen months. The potty chair was not set off in the bathroom, it was part of the main activity of the house. I either placed it in the kitchen or living room. I moved it around, depending on where everyone was spending their time. Some high chairs even had a hole with a little pot to catch pee or poop as a child sat to eat a meal.

Just as my girls pretended to feed and put their dollies to bed, they set their dolls and Teddy bears on the potty chair and played toileting. I never asked my girls if they needed to use the toilet. Every hour or so (more often when I started) I just set them on the potty chair and told them to pee. Sometimes they would, sometimes they wouldn't; eventually they caught on. Yes, each child had accidents, but once diapers were removed and training pants put on, I never brought out the diapers again.

I didn't question my toilet training practices. I just did it like everyone else. I devoted lots of time, attention, and energy to toilet training. It wasn't something I just hoped would happen.

My first child was trained at eighteen months, the second a little later. The third was earlier than the first two because of all the coaching and assistance she received from her older sisters.

I definitely think mothers wait too long and are too relaxed today about toilet training. My granddaughter wasn't trained until two and a half, and she still wears a diaper at night.

In days past, most mothers, like Jackie, were home all day to care for their children. Consequently when it was time to train, the day could revolve around the toileting process. Today, guiding a child to use the toilet is interrupted by busy schedules that often involve more than one caregiver. Mom, Grandma, Dad, and a child care provider may all be involved in training. Understandably, this can confuse the child and delay the process.

If conflict develops between parents or caregivers, it needs to be resolved before you can proceed with training. If one adult is more easygoing and another more determined to get the task accomplished, a middle ground needs to be established so the child won't be unnecessarily confused and frustrated.

Historically, teaching a child to use the toilet was defined differently. A child was considered trained when Mom took her child to the toilet and he performed at her request. Also, Mom was in tune with and carefully watched her child's body language just prior to urinating or having a bowel movement. When she noticed any pre-urinating or pre-bowel movement signals from the child, she'd quickly snatch the child and transport him off to the toilet.

Today's parents are usually unavailable for this intense monitoring. Now a child is considered trained when he comes to the parent and says, "I need to pee," and the parent then takes him to the toilet. Yesterday it was the parent's accomplishment, today it's the child's.

It's also important to remember Grandma didn't have the lavish laundry facilities of today, disposable diapers, or a diaper service. Early potty training meant less time spent doing laundry.

The differences of past and present make it irrelevant to argue that one approach is better than the other. We live in a different world today: parents have the luxury of low maintenance diapers and laundry; the focus on toilet training is the child's achievement, not the mother's; and parents know it's impossible to truly train until the child is physically able to hold in the urine and stool and then release it. Now parents brag about how little Johnny trained himself with only some minor guidance from his mom and dad.

TODAY'S PITFALLS

As a result of today's child-centered approach, however, some parents relax *too* much and wait for the child to train himself. They don't nudge their child even a little because they fear it will leave psychological scars. Some parents don't encourage their child to use the toilet even when the child displays most of the readiness signs. Their lives are stressful enough without adding potty training. Diapers are so convenient, it's easy to let toilet training wait. Other parents get into potty problems because they don't take time to adequately orient their child to the toileting process. The result is a delay of training and some children even become resistant to the toileting process altogether.

Stories from the Bathroom

❥ Sam's mom, Judy, was afraid to push training, hoping somehow it would miraculously occur. When Sam turned two, she bought a potty seat. Sam sat on it once but didn't appear interested. At three, Sam still isn't trained and Judy is wondering what to do. Power struggles occur daily because Judy has lost her patience; it's time for Sam to train and he refuses to cooperate.

Judy is not alone in her predicament. Parents today can avoid these struggles if they start to familiarize their children early toward toileting procedures.

DEALING WITH CRITICISM

Grandma claims resistance to training or laziness on the part of the parent was unheard of in her day. It's not necessary for either generation to prove one approach is right or wrong. What's important is to borrow techniques from Grandma that can work today, and combine those with what we know about a child's development to best toilet train children.

It's okay for grandparents who don't approve of how their children are training their grandchildren to explain how they went about the process themselves. But that advice should only be offered once. Toilet training can be a frustrating and emotionally-charged process; adult children need the support of their parents, not criticism.

When you approach toileting instruction differently than your mother, she might conclude you think the way she trained you was wrong. Be sensitive to this and don't argue. When she gives her opinion, listen, nod, thank her for her advice, and then train your child the way you think is best. There's no need to get defensive; a battle with your mother about toilet training is a waste of time and energy.

Here's all you need to say to anyone from an earlier generation who offers unsolicited advice, "Boy, teaching a child to use the toilet is certainly different today. It's interesting to hear how you accomplished the task. I appreciate your ideas."

Borrow from Grandma her enthusiasm, determination, and skill, take into account your child's developmental readiness, and then apply both to the process of toilet training. The goal: children eager and interested to use the toilet so when they're physically able, they'll be willing and excited to perform.

AVOID THE HARD-LINE APPROACH

One fact remains the same for yesterday and today: Force, pressure, threats, and verbal or physical abuse only hurt the child's emotional well-being and delay the toilet training process.

Avoid coercive tactics like this: "All your friends will be going to preschool in the fall. But not you, because you're not potty trained." A parent might say this hoping it will motivate her child to train. More frequently, it only leaves the child confused. Preschool is an unfamiliar experience to a child; it will occur sometime in the future, but the child really doesn't understand when. Warnings about staying home from lack of toileting ability can leave the child wondering, "What's wrong with staying home?" or not knowing how to advance in his skills. It's better to develop a plan for steering your child to use the toilet rather than making threats.

Another manipulative statement is, "Big boys go in the toilet; babies pee and poop in diapers. Are you going to be a baby all your life?" Parents use this line to encourage their child to mature and use the toilet, but it usually backfires. Children already feel torn between growing up and staying little; this statement only adds to their dilemma.

Stories from the Bathroom

👣 Zach, age two, refused to poop in the toilet. Dad actually tied him to the toilet and told him to sit there until he pooped. Zach sat an hour, crying and screaming, but didn't have a bowel movement. Finally, Dad untied Zach; fortunately he realized this was abusive and unproductive to toilet training.

In the past, some mothers were more than determined when it came to directing their children to use the toilet. Some would spank and scream at their children to bring results on the toilet. According to Alison Mack's book *Toilet Learning*[1], many incidents of child abuse center around toilet training. Toileting instruction sometimes becomes a battle of wills between parent and child. The parent is certain the child can poop on the toilet but for some unknown reason won't. The child's willfulness triggers the parent's anger and the parent threatens the child, "If you don't poop on that toilet I'll spank you." The child refuses and the parent carries out the threat. This same scenario played out

---

[1]Mack, Alison. *Toilet Learning.* Little, Brown & Co. 1978.

several times a day with escalating anger and more severe spankings equates to child abuse.

WHO'S REALLY IN CONTROL?

There is a lot a parent can do to influence toileting success but ultimately, control lies with the child. Just as parents can't force a child to eat or sleep, they can't force a child to use the toilet.

For bowel training some mothers of the past generation used glycerine suppositories on their young children. At the same time each day, Mother inserted the suppository, waited thirty minutes or so and then put the child on the toilet. This created a predictable bowel schedule, which in turn meant no more dirty diapers. This process would now be unthinkable. Today's parents want the toilet training process to occur as naturally as possible.

Stories from the Bathroom

❦ Debbie, mother of two-year-old Megan, was determined to have Megan trained by her second birthday. Grandma was coming to visit and Debbie wanted to show off her skill as a mom and the cooperativeness of her daughter.

Little Megan was eager to please. She wore her panties proudly and remained dry, but only peed in the toilet once or twice a day at Debbie's request. Megan knew how to hold her urine in, but hadn't developed to the point mentally or physically where she could release it when her bladder was full. Mom waited for Megan to tell her she needed to go, but she didn't. Finally, a couple of times a day, Mom would set her on her little toilet seat and tell her to go. At night, when Megan finally relaxed, she wet her bed thoroughly. This set up a pattern that continued until she was six.

Debbie could claim Megan was trained, but she paid for this early declaration with years of unnecessary bed wetting. If she had waited until Megan had developed physically just a little bit more, she may have been able to prevent those years of bed wetting.

THE BALANCE BETWEEN GENERATIONS

The pressure and time some mothers focused on early training in years past was significant. Many mothers felt an urgency to train and applied pressure to their children. Parents today want to avoid this tension. It is clear the pendulum has swung. Today, toileting is viewed as the child's accomplishment—so training is now more low-key and relaxed. For most parents and children this approach works just fine; children train somewhere between two and three years old. The flip side is that some parents go too far with the laid-back approach, do too little, and miss the "window of opportunity" for training. Then when they do insist the child train, they meet with a great deal of resistance. Children sense when a parent is tense or ambivalent when it comes to toilet training. Such was the case with Michael in the story below.

Stories from the Bathroom

❦ Michelle was confused; she knew not to push her child to use the toilet, so ended up doing nothing in fear of doing something wrong. She waited and hoped Michael would just train himself. The toilet became a novelty item he avoided. The result: Michael side-stepped the toilet and training until well into his third year, beyond what was necessary.

Michael was Michelle's first child so she was understandably unsure about how to approach training. Finally she mustered up the courage, exuded confidence, hid her anxieties, and set aside time each day for underpants, accidents, and toileting instruction. It was a few short days before Michael was in underpants full time.

Where's the middle ground? What can parents learn from Grandma that will assist training in a timely manner when the child is physically and mentally ready? Parents today will probably never go back to Grandma's way, but they can learn from the past.

Borrow the enthusiasm, but don't apply the pressure of Grandma's day. Incorporate a low level of determination. But remember, don't be too relaxed; guiding a child to use the toilet doesn't always miraculously occur. There's much you can do to lay the groundwork for successful training. Be careful not to let your child's window of opportunity for training slip by.

What's required from you is the knowledge of how and when to encourage your child. Combine this with an alertness to recognize the signs described in Chapter 1 for developmental readiness. Keep in mind early training is not the goal, *timely* training is.

GOOD IDEAS FROM GRANDMA

Here are some ideas adapted from Grandma's approach that will be useful to you today.

☑ Starting at about eighteen months, take your child with you when you use the toilet. Talk about what you're doing and let the child flush when you're done.

☑ At two years old, buy or borrow a potty chair. Have the potty chair in the main living area of the house. Move it around from room to room. This way, your child has the opportunity to become familiar with the potty chair. It won't be some foreign object set off in the bathroom.

☑ Encourage your child to put dollies and Teddy bears on the toilet. Realize that your child comes to understand "this potty business" through play.

☑ When you go to use the toilet, take your child and her potty chair with you. Encourage her to sit on her toilet. (Don't take her diaper off and don't expect any performance at first. You're just getting your child familiar with the toileting process.) Give her a book to look at or a toy to hold. If your child won't sit at first, set a doll on the toilet and talk about how the doll is peeing in the toilet.

☑ Put your child on the toilet twice a day, after breakfast and as part of the bedtime routine. At first, keep diapers on. Later, take them off and then eventually, ask your child to pee or poop. Don't ask your child if he wants to sit on the toilet, just take him. Offer a choice if necessary, "Do you want to look at a book or hold your doll when you sit on the potty seat?" Be persistent and consistent. Don't be forceful, just firm and kind. Use an inviting tone of voice, "Oh yes, remember, we *always* sit on the toilet after breakfast." Children like a consistent routine, so if you forget, your child will soon be reminding you.

☑ Focus attention on your child whenever she or he shows interest in the toilet. Be enthusiastic about any minor success. Talk about and describe your child's involvement in toileting. "Look at Teddy, he's sitting on the toilet going potty." "You peed in the toilet, good for you."

Use these tips so your child is eager and interested to start the toileting process. The next chapter gives you a place to start.

3

A PLACE TO START

You're ready to train your child, and you sense your child is ready too. But how do you officially begin? Do you just take the diapers away, put your son in underpants, and hope for the best? Do you wait for your daughter to suddenly announce, "I don't like those diapers anymore, I want big girl pants now." Or do you dress your child in underpants part time and train in small steps?

The truth is, there is no one perfectly prescribed plan for guiding your child to use the toilet. Some children literally train themselves, not wanting any assistance or coaching. Others are reluctant and ignore any potty training plan you might impose, then seem to miraculously train in their own way and time. Most ease into using the toilet with guidance, encouragement, and a plan imposed flexibly by parents or child care providers.

FINDING TIME

An important ingredient required for training is time. Be prepared to set aside some of your regular activities because you'll need extra energy to take on potty training. Teaching your child to use the toilet requires you to carefully and quietly monitor your child's progress.

Stories from the Bathroom

❥ Sandi was a busy mom. She had a two year old and a new baby, plus worked part time, volunteered for community projects, managed her home, shopped, exercised, and entertained. One Seattle winter it snowed for a week. Sandi was housebound, so her life was forced to slow down. That week she trained her daughter Cassie. Two years later a windstorm hit Seattle; parts of the city were shut down without power for five long days. Again, Sandi was housebound. That week she trained her two-year-old son.

UNDERPANTS AND POTTY CHAIRS

Start by making two purchases. First, take your child to buy underwear or panties. There are many cute ones on the market. Previously, the underwear trend was superhero designs for the boys, and ruffles, lace, and bows for the girls. Today, it tends to be Disney characters. Who knows what or who will decorate the underwear of tomorrow, but it's fun and important to involve your child by letting him or her pick out these new underpants.

What about thick training pants or the disposable training diapers that children pull up like underpants? Many parents use them because they're a convenient way to bridge the transition from diapers to a thinner panty. They absorb the urine and hold up the stool, so if your child has an accident less mess ends up on the floor.

There is a drawback, however—they're too much like diapers. The child in training doesn't get the sensation of going or needing to go because their bottoms are padded with all that thick material. Buy them if they are helpful to you, but understand that once toileting instruction is underway, the thinner cloth variety will be more useful for learning the difference between the sensations of wet and dry, and messy and clean.

Second, purchase a potty chair that is placed on the floor or a seat that fits on the rim of the big toilet. If you choose the latter, you'll need to set your child on the seat until she is big enough to climb up there by herself, or purchase one that includes steps.

Some parents prefer the little potty chair that sits on the floor because the child is often inspired to try toileting at the same time Mom or Dad uses the big toilet. Also, most children do better for bowel movements when they have a place to put their feet. It's more difficult to push out stool if your feet are dangling. The drawback is that you must clean the removable pot each time the child urinates or has a bowel movement. This task is only temporary, however, as children soon advance to the household toilet.

Buy either a toilet seat or a potty chair, but realize your child may have some distinct ideas about which he'll use.

Stories from the Bathroom

❥ Janie bought a potty chair that sits on the floor for her son, Max. Then Aunt Betsy brought over the variety that sits on the big toilet—the one she used with her children. Max had a choice; he could use the potty rim on the big toilet, or he could use the potty chair. Max liked neither. He was determined to use the big toilet just like Mom and his big brother. He would balance there for bowel movements and to urinate. He never fell into the toilet, much to his mother and brother's amazement.

GETTING STARTED

The magical moment for potty training to officially begin is difficult to determine. Trust your intuition. You've watched your child develop daily from birth. You're tuned in to your child's readiness to take on any new challenge. So trust yourself, observe your child, and if you know the time is right, begin.

Don't start because you're feeling pressure from friends and relatives. Begin because all the signs point to the fact that the time is right for your child and you. If you're not sure, re-read the "Readiness Checklist" at the end of Chapter 1.

Here's a sample plan to get you started. Many parents have used this procedure. As you progress, you will find your own path to finish the process.

Step One: Practice

The toileting process begins with practice, not performance. You can compare it to eating. Think about how strange it would be to your child if you nursed or bottle-fed him until he was two and a half and then suddenly you set him in the high chair and expected him to eat solid food three times a day. The child would be baffled and resistant. Of course, parents don't do this. We gradually introduce solid foods and independent eating and eventually wean children from the breast and the bottle. Many of the meals in the high chair end up being only practice sessions because children often play with the food and eat very little.

The same approach applies to toilet training. Parents gradually introduce the potty and eventually eliminate diapers. Children need lots of opportunities for rehearsing the toileting procedure along the way.

Some children just naturally show interest in using the

toilet. There is no need to impose a practice routine on the child who takes the initiative to rehearse on his own.

If your child is not already in the habit of sitting on the toilet seat or potty chair to practice using the potty, now is the time to establish this habit. Remember, children thrive on consistency and routine. To begin, choose two routine times to familiarize your child with toileting and stick with these times. (Children often respond well when you nickname these sessions "Poo-Poo Time.") These trips to the toilet could be before getting dressed, before lunch, before bathtime, after dinner, or before bedtime.

If your child has shown little interest in toileting, you might need to impose a routine on these practice sessions. Don't take diapers off at first unless your child is willing. Further, don't expect your child to perform. This is only practice and working toileting into your daily routine. Also, don't ask your child, "Do you want to sit on the toilet?" Your child could very well say, "No." Instead, use a firm, friendly, and clear approach: "Oh remember, we have a new rule, we *always* sit on the toilet before getting dressed." Even if your child is a little reluctant, don't hesitate; proceed with confidence.

Stories from the Bathroom

❥ Jennifer put a basket of little books in the bathroom. She'd entice Wesley this way, "It's Poo-Poo Time. You can choose one book for me to read to you while you sit there."

Another technique is to have your child carry a toy with him to the bathroom. Use this line, "Remember, we always sit on the potty before lunch—would you like to take your truck with you?"

It's essential to be clear about the importance of these visits to the toilet. Use a purposeful voice as you walk your child to the bathroom. Then once your child is on the toilet or potty chair, make it a pleasant time for you and your child to be together. Surround your child with love and nurture. Sing songs. Tell stories. Be at your parenting best here. You want your child to have pleasant associations with toileting procedures.

Think of the interest, love, patience, and guidance you focused on your child when she learned to walk. That's the same interest and support your child needs as she learns to use the toilet. Notice and describe each minor success along the way. "Good for you, you're grunting, you're trying to push out a poop." Jumping up and down with praise is less important than carefully describing each minor success and focusing on your child with adoring looks as she sits on the toilet.

Stories from the Bathroom

❥ Phyllis wanted to start Lisa, age two and a half, on the road to toileting. She'd ask Lisa, "Do you want to sit on the potty?" Lisa's consistent reply was, "No." But then Phyllis realized Lisa was saying "No" to most everything: ice cream, play school, going to the park—all things she really enjoyed. So Phyllis stopped asking and just started taking her to the bathroom. At first she would kick and scream as her mother confidently carried her to the bathroom. Phyllis would sit Lisa on the toilet, lovingly hold her there and say encouragingly, "Someday you'll pee and poop in the toilet." Soon Lisa was automatically sitting on the toilet each morning before climbing into the bathtub.

The mother in the above story realized her daughter wasn't specifically resisting toilet training, she was resisting the change being imposed on her life. This child adjusted to the potty sitting time after three short days. If after a week your child continues to resist, you might consider waiting a bit and re-introducing the potty sitting time again in a month.

Step Two: Potty-Sitting Time Without Diapers

After your child is in the routine of sitting on the potty at least twice a day, remove the diapers for the potty sitting time.   Don't expect any success yet but speak in encouraging terms: "Someday you'll pee and poop in this potty just like Mom, Dad, and sister. Right now you're just practicing."

Expect your child to protest.   Since you're probably steering your child to use the toilet somewhere between the ages of two and three years old, your child will protest *any* rules you impose.   This is normal two-year-old behavior. It's a fine line parents walk here; you want to be firm and kind, but not harsh or forceful.   Remember, your child will feel competent and grown-up when she can pee and poop into the toilet.   You're just helping the process along.

Accept your child's feelings and then proceed matter-of-factly.   "I know you don't want to take your diapers off and sit on the toilet, but remember, we *always* sit on the toilet before leaving the house and now we must practice with your diapers off."   If your child only sits there for two seconds, praise her. "Good for you, you sat on the toilet." Don't plead for more cooperation, don't shrug your shoulders and act defeated.   She sat there for two seconds— next time she'll probably sit longer.

Step Three: Underpants

Once your child is in the habit of practicing sitting on the toilet without diapers, put on underpants for a two-hour period of time each day.   This is a big step.   Parents proceed differently from this point. Three useful approaches are described beginning on page 32. Most parents get daytime training established and then move on to night training. However you decide to continue, and with whatever techniques, you must be prepared for accidents.

TOILETING ACCIDENTS

It's unrealistic to think your child will never wet or poop in his colorful new underpants. When children accidently poop or pee in their underwear it helps them recognize the sensation of "going." When a child realizes that he is pooping or peeing at the moment, then it follows he will soon be able to read the signals from his body that tell him he is *needing* to go. Accidents are an important part of making this body-to-mind connection.

A child must feel what it's like to actually go before he can thoughtfully control the bowel and bladder muscles long enough to reach the toilet. When children finally make this connection you will see it written all over their faces.

Stories from the Bathroom

〉 Carter stood on a chair at the kitchen table completing a puzzle, new underpants on, but that's all—no shoes, socks or pants.

All of the sudden he started to pee. His eyes lighted up, he gasped and looked down to see pee running down his leg. Mom calmly responded, "Carter, you're peeing. Let's go in the bathroom, so you can sit on the toilet. I'll clean you up." After Mom cleaned him, she set him on the toilet and said, "Next time when you feel the need to pee, tell me and I'll take you in the bathroom so you can pee in the toilet."

After this experience Carter knew what Mom was talking about. He still had a few accidents, but each day there were fewer.

CLEANING UP AFTER ACCIDENTS

Bowel accidents are messier to clean up. If your child poops in his underwear, clean him in the bathtub. Remove the soiled clothing and explain calmly, "Next time you need to poop, tell me and I'll take you to sit on the toilet."

After an accident and you've cleaned your child up, it helps if you can get him to sit on the potty seat or chair for a minute or so. By doing this you're helping your child make the connection that poop and pee go into the toilet. Read your child a story* about going potty, make up a silly peeing and pooping song and sing it, or tell your child a story you've made up about a little boy who used to pee and poop in his underpants but now goes in the toilet.

Stories from the Bathroom

❥ Janet didn't want Alex to have accidents and experience any toileting failure; she only wanted him to have success. He was bowel trained completely, but continued to pee in his diapers. As Alex approached three years old, Janet didn't know what step to take next so Alex could learn to urinate in the toilet while avoiding any accidents. She consulted a child development specialist who assured her it would not damage Alex's self-esteem to have a few accidents. In fact, he needed to experience the sensation of peeing without diapers to get the idea of what this urinating business was all about.

Once training begins, don't be horrified by accidents. Be prepared for them. Corn starch dries up wet pee spots on carpets, chairs, and mattresses. If your child is sitting on

---

*Refer to the list of recommended children's books on potty training at the end of this book.

the couch and wets his underpants, just put lots of corn starch on the spot, let it dry overnight, and vacuum it up the next day.

When you take your newly-trained child in the car, always take an extra set of clothes with you. Many children won't pee in strange toilets at shopping malls and restaurants. They only want to pee in their very own toilet. Some parents take a portable potty seat with them during this period. Other parents point out the restroom when they arrive and remind the child, "We can go potty here, even though we aren't at home."

It won't be too long, however, before your son or daughter will want to try out every toilet available, whether you're at a friend's house or a gas station.

Also be prepared when your newly-trained child says she needs to go—you don't have much time. You can't ask your child to wait while you finish your shopping; you must locate a restroom right then. In time, the bowel and bladder muscles strengthen to the point where the child can hold the urine and stool in for longer periods, but at first the waiting period is very short.

THREE TRAINING APPROACHES

Here are three techniques parents find useful once a child has progressed past the three beginning steps recommended earlier in the chapter.

Approach Number One: Part-time Potty Training

One approach is to set aside a convenient two-hour period during each day for toileting education. During this time the child wears underpants. Your job is to take your child to the toilet after the first hour to encourage him to perform. If the child stays dry and clean and performs on the toilet, gradually extend the time he wears underpants until he has them on all day long.

Stories from the Bathroom

❥ This approach worked for Mike, a busy single dad who was encouraging Eric to use the toilet. Eric was in a variety of child care settings—sometimes with Mom, Grandma, or in a family child care. It was too complicated to coordinate with all of them, so Mike decided that when he and Eric were home together in the evening, he'd put Eric in underpants.

Eric resisted—he liked his diapers. After all, he'd worn them since infancy. When Mike tried to talk him into wearing his big-boy underwear, Eric stomped his foot and said "No way." Mike backed off until the next night.

Then he tried this tactic: "Eric, there's a new rule in this house. It states: When Eric and Dad are home together, Eric wears underwear." Eric looked at his dad a little stunned, but complied. At first he had a few accidents, but after three days he seldom wet his pants and always pooped in the toilet

After a week Mike put Eric in underwear full time. At each child care setting Mike informed the caregiver of Eric's new toileting skill. There were some accidents as each child care provider worked with him, but soon he was successful no matter where he was.

Approach Number Two: Child's Choice Method

Some parents give their child a choice. They ask the child if she wants to wear diapers or underpants. This is a good technique to use if there's an emotional power struggle brewing between parent and child. Having some say in the matter helps the child feel more in control of the process.

Stories from the Bathroom

❩ Mary used this technique with Liesel. Every morning she would ask, "Do you want to wear underpants or diapers today?" Some days Liesel would choose diapers, other days underpants. After a week Liesel wasn't having any accidents when she wore underpants. So when the disposable diapers ran out, Mary just told her, "The diapers are all gone. I'm not buying more at the store." Liesel didn't protest; she was ready for underpants full time.

Approach Number Three: Full-time Potty Training

Many parents bite the bullet and put their child in underpants full time. This takes a lot of time and attention from the parent, but works for many families.

Stories from the Bathroom

❩ This was Angela's approach. Adam was close to three years old. He had practiced peeing and pooping on the toilet, liked to set his favorite Teddy on the toilet and pretend about toileting, frequently watched Dad in the bathroom, was telling Mom regularly when he was wet or his diapers were full, and he was clean for long periods during the day. Mom had prepared him for the official beginning of training, "You know, next Monday you won't be wearing diapers anymore, you'll be wearing underpants just like Dad." They marked the days off on the calendar.

So the day came. At first Adam protested, "No, I want my diapers." But Mom insisted, "Remember, I told you, today you're going to wear your dinosaur underwear." With an unhappy face Adam put on his underwear. He had several accidents the first day, fewer the next, and in five days his accidents dwindled to one or two a week. After a month he was trained.

WORKING WITH YOUR CHILD CARE PROVIDER

If your child is in child care, you need the support and cooperation of your provider in order to train your child. There are four areas to pay attention to.

Communication

If you sense your child is ready for toilet training, communicate with your provider first. Does she agree? What's her approach? How can she help? As your child works toward using the toilet, talk each day about his or her successes and setbacks.

Cooperation

If your provider initiates the training, or if your child shows interest at the care center because all of the other kids use the potty, go along with her suggestions and approach. Follow through at home with a similar program.

Collaboration

Many providers include potty training in their daily routine for children two-to-three years old. Find out your provider's approach. If you have different potty training ideas, discuss these differences. Don't conference at the door; call her when the kids nap, in the evening, or on the weekend. If necessary, set up an appointment.

Consideration

Potty training can be frustrating for providers who care for multi-aged children. If your child has lots of accidents in the child care setting, be sure to provide lots of underpants and extra clothes. You might need to do laundry daily. Purchase a potty seat for your child to use at child care if your provider doesn't have one. Do what you can to support your caregiver through the potty training process.

MORE TIPS FOR TOILETING SUCCESS

Here are some ideas and tips that will help smooth the road to toilet training.

Watch the Liquids

If a child drinks lots of liquids from a bottle, it might be harder to train that child to urinate in the toilet. It just makes sense that the less liquid a child ingests, the easier the bladder will be to control. Don't dehydrate your child, but keep an eye on how much he's drinking.

Reminders

When you first put your child in underwear, you might offer a reminder every hour or so. "Son, do you need to pee? Let's try. I'll go with you to the bathroom." But be careful because your child may get into the habit of depending on you to tell him when it's time to go. Eventually your child must learn to read his own body signals to discover the sensation of needing to go. So at first ask, "Do you feel like you need to pee or poop?" Later, back off and allow your child to take on the responsibility of the toileting process himself without reminders from you.

Boys

Do they stand up or sit down to urinate? Some boys want to stand up just like Dad and big brother. Some begin by sitting down and pushing their penises down into the toilet so the pee hits the toilet bowl rather than the floor. You must show or demonstrate this to your son.

Boys who begin by sitting soon copy Dad who stands to pee. Others learn from observing neighborhood pals or bigger boys at preschool or child care. Some boys sit facing the back of the toilet to start and then eventually stand.

Girls

Little girls sometimes pee too far forward and wet on their panties. Help your daughter place herself far enough back on the seat to get the pee in the toilet. Help her slide her panties all the way down to her ankles. In time and with practice, she will discover a comfortable and efficient position for urinating.

Clothing

Don't dress your child in clothes that are difficult to get out of: jeans with a zipper, belts, snaps, jumpsuits, or overalls. Make it easy on your child to get pants up and down quickly with as little assistance from you as possible. Some parents dress their children in sweat pants for training with no underwear on at all. This makes it easy to get pants down quickly. Girls in dresses have it easy because they can lift up their dresses and pull down their panties quickly. Some parents let children run around naked so they are not encumbered at all.

Urine vs. Bowel Training

Some children bowel train first, others urine train first and some learn to do both at the same time. Realize that if your child learns to do one before the other, this is not unusual. Bowel and bladder muscles are different. They are in different locations and offer a different set of needing-to-go sensations. So watch your child and if you see he's having success peeing in the toilet, don't pressure him to learn to poop there too. Let him accomplish urine training first and then take on bowel training. For example, two-and-a-half-year-old Elizabeth learned to pee in the toilet first. A week after she was confidently completing this task, her mom introduced bowel training.

Cleanliness

Children need to learn hygienic habits when it comes to using the toilet. They need to sit or stand carefully so the urine and stool reaches the toilet. Eventually they must learn to wipe themselves, but at first they need assistance from you—especially for bowel movements. For girls, teach them to wipe themselves from front to back, in order to avoid introducing bacteria into the vagina.

Children need to learn to flush and then wash their hands afterwards. It may be a hassle to enforce, but it is an important habit to instill. The most effective approach is for parent and child to wash their hands together. Insist on good hygiene, but don't obsess about it. Some parents are so overly fastidious about germs that their children begin retaining their bowels to avoid all the fuss.

Gimmicks

There are a variety of tricks you can use to make toileting more fun for kids.

▪   You can buy targets to float in the toilet. These entice boys not only to pee into the toilet but it helps improve their aim.

▪   If you put blue food coloring in the toilet, it will turn green as your child pees. Some children think this is magical.

▪   Engage the child's imagination. For example, Grandma excitedly said to her grandson as he was in the process of training, "Jerry, there's a fire in the toilet, you better run and put it out." Jerry's face lit up and his imagination took over. For that moment he was a fire fighter. He ran into the bathroom and peed, pretending to be at the scene of a big fire.

Jessica named her poops. The big ones were daddy poops, the middle-sized ones were mommy poops, and the tiny ones were baby poops. She'd wave "bye-bye" to her family of poops as she flushed them down the toilet.

Sally loved her Barney the Dinosaur® panties. Her mom made this remark, "Sally, now remember, you don't want to get any pee or poop on Barney." When Sally had an accident, Mom said calmly, "Oh, no, you pooped on Barney. He doesn't like poop on him and hopes you'll poop in the toilet next time." Mom was careful not to shame Sally, but her comment helped motivate Sally to toileting success.

All of these gimmicks may sound silly to adults, but to children (who have wonderful imaginations) they're not outrageous or coercive at all. So tap into your child's imagination; it will help.

Bathroom Talk

Don't be surprised if you hear your child use words that refer to urine and stool in inappropriate ways and in inappropriate settings. This is common practice among children up to about age five. "He's a poo-poo head." "This soup looks like pee." The variations on the use of these words are only limited by a child's imagination which, during the preschool years, is fertile and unbridled. If your child notices that this talk bothers you a great deal, it usually only gets worse. Many parent's emotions are easily triggered by the inappropriate and over-use of references to bodily functions.

If bathroom talk does cause a persistent problem, each time your child uses it, nonchalantly escort him to the bathroom. Tell him, "If you need to use bathroom talk, the place to use it is in the bathroom." When you get there, sit down and tell your child that you will listen. Don't act shocked, just listen and when your child is finished, ask him, "Are you finished using bathroom talk now? If you need to use those words again, let me know. I'll come to the bathroom with you any time to listen." This approach defuses the negative attention such words can bring. Bathroom talk quickly drops out of sight—at least in your presence.

ONE PARENT'S TRAINING STORY

Chelsey's habit was to pee in the toilet every evening before climbing into the bathtub. It was part of the evening routine.

Her mom, Nikki, wanted Chelsey trained and felt at two and a half she was developmentally ready. Grandma was visiting so Nikki saw this as the perfect time; Grandma would be there for moral support and to care for Chelsey's younger brother while Nikki was training Chelsey or cleaning up accidents. Here's Nikki's story:

> One morning when we woke up I just said, "Today you're going to wear the princess underwear we bought at the store." I let Chelsey pick out the pair she liked best and we put them on her. She had accidents all day long—at least seven. As the day went on, she'd start to pee, notice it, and then run to the bathroom to finish in the potty chair. I let her do this without asking if she had to go because I didn't want her to get dependent on me for reminders. She began making progress on her own.

The second day we went to the shopping center. Chelsey announced she had to go, but by the time we found a toilet she was soaked. After I cleaned her up, I set her on the toilet for a minute anyway.

Chelsey didn't like to be wet or dirty so I think that helped a lot. We did bowel training and urine training at the same time. Believe me, the first two days were a mess. We just dealt with it. She urine trained easiest. Then one day I found her busy putting her dolls on and off the potty chair having them grunt and pretend to poop. She'd wipe one and then put another on. The next day she pooped in the toilet for the first time and only had a couple of accidents after this.

I did give her rewards: a sticker for peeing in the toilet and a lollipop for pooping. One time she was grunting and trying to force out a poop just to get that lollipop. I said, "Mommy doesn't want you to push; Mommy wants you to wait until it's ready." This little bit of coaching took care of the problem. If I got frustrated, my mom would say to me, "It's okay. She's learning. Remember, she's only two." This support really helped me through those tense moments.

If Chelsey went a little in her panties but then made it to the bathroom to finish in the toilet, she'd still get a sticker. She was completely trained in five days. I was so pleased.

GETTING STARTED CHECKLIST

If your child is ready physically, emotionally, socially, and intellectually, start by:

☑ Setting aside a block of time in your busy life to begin training.

☑ Taking your child to buy underwear.

☑ Buying a potty chair or a ring to fit on the big toilet.

☑ Establishing two potty-sitting practice sessions a day. Leave diapers on. (This step is necessary only if your child isn't naturally interested in toileting.)

Do these above four steps simultaneously.

If your child is cooperative, proceed by:

☑ Taking diapers off for practice sessions, but don't expect performance.

If your child continues to cooperate and her interest is piqued, proceed by choosing one of the following three options:

☑ Part-time Potty Training

Put on underpants for a two-hour period each day. Take your child to the toilet to try peeing and pooping after the first hour. If the child stays dry and clean, and performs on the potty, gradually extend the time in underpants until the child is completely trained.

☑ Child's Choice Method

Let the child choose each day between diapers or underpants. On the underpants days note how many accidents occur and if they diminish. Eventually, when you sense the time is right, end the diaper-wearing option.

☑ Full-time Potty Training

The parent feels the child is ready for underpants full-time, warns the child one week prior to the event and begins on the designated day. The parent is prepared for accidents, assumes a matter-of-fact demeanor, and notices if the child gradually catches on to using the toilet full-time.

The time frame for achieving training success is difficult to determine. Some children experience immediate success—after a week they are confident toilet users. Other children make slower, but definite progress. If after a month your child still has lots of accidents, it's time to re-evaluate his readiness, possibly return to diapers, and allow him a little more time to mature.

4

WHEN YOUR PLAN FOR TRAINING DOESN'T SUCCEED

Sometimes, for any variety of reasons, your attempts to toilet train your child are not successful. Even though you have read many child-focused toilet training books to your child, placed a potty chair in your bathroom, and purchased cute Disney underwear for her, she has accident after accident.

Days go by and still there's no toileting successes. You try rewarding her with candy, but she's not interested. You try sitting her on the toilet every hour and she's willing to try, but ends up tense, in tears, and never manages to get one drop in the toilet. Then, minutes later, her underpants are wet again.

Despite the fact you thought she was ready physically, emotionally, intellectually, and socially—after all she is two and a half—it's clear she just isn't ready. If, after a week of struggles and accidents, you don't observe any progress or interest from your child, back off, put diapers back on, and try again in a couple of months.

If your child is slow to catch on but you sense he is making baby steps toward training, keep at it. Consistent control just takes longer for some children than others. Your child may require more time to perceive the sensation of needing to go and may need a longer time to strengthen the bowel and bladder muscles. Putting the child who is making gradual progress back in diapers would spell defeat and negate any minor successes the child experienced.

Before returning your child to diapers, notice your child's body type. Does he or she appear to have an overall muscular physique that is tight and quick to respond? Or does your child have a more relaxed muscular appearance and physique? Children whose muscles are taut gain almost instantaneous control of their bowel and bladder muscles. Others with loose muscles need more time to respond. If relaxed muscles is one of your child's physical characteristics, then toileting instruction may take a little longer. This is one reason why some children need only a week to catch on, and others take a month or more.

When your child is in diapers she may squat to urinate or have a bowel movement. Other children may sit in a chair, or stand. Another child may have a bowel movement only when relaxed after a nap or right after a bath. When you start educating your child to use the toilet, you are introducing a new environment: Suddenly, she is required to sit on the toilet, without diapers, and poop or pee. The difference in surroundings and positions takes some adjustment on your child's part. So be patient as your child learns to use his or her muscles in a new way and in a new place. Both boys and girls must figure out how to get their muscles to push out pee and poop into the toilet and this may be quite different from their old diaper-protected positions.

Some children have a difficult time relaxing. This was the case in the following story.

Stories from the Bathroom

❱ Jimmy insisted on standing to pee, but he'd just stand there and stand there; he could never relax enough to pee in the toilet. Mom and Dad knew Jimmy had physical control because he'd wake up dry each morning.

Jimmy's morning routine was to wake up and sit on his mom's lap for a story. One morning his mom said, "I'll read you your story while you stand at the toilet and try to pee." That's all it took. As she read Jimmy the story, he finally relaxed and peed into the toilet.

IGNORING THE MESSAGE

Once schooling a child to use the toilet is officially underway, it usually takes only three or four days to sense if your child is catching on to the training regime. After a month, the process should be fairly well organized.

It's difficult for children to focus on their play activity *and* listen to their body's messages about the need to go. Some children playing outside don't want to miss out on any fun so they put off trips to the bathroom for too long. They don't give themselves enough time to run inside and end up wetting their pants. Some boys remedy this easily by sneaking off to pee behind a tree; for girls, this approach is less convenient, so they usually learn to run into the house for quick trips to the bathroom.

Most children do need reminders. Occasionally parents get in the habit of too frequently reminding their child about visiting the bathroom, and then escorting their child there to urinate or have a bowel movement. This is okay to begin with, but if you continue to take your child to the toilet and frequently remind your child about visiting the bathroom, at some point you need to back off and let him assume this responsibility himself. He needs to listen to the signals from his body that tell him it's time to go. Yes, he might have an accident or two, but that's typically all it takes to master the process.

A TEMPORARY RETURN TO DIAPERS

If you ease off and your child doesn't take over the responsibility of toileting, consider putting diapers back on and make another attempt in a couple of months.

Remember, Grandma never returned her children to diapers because this would have spelled embarrassment, failure, and humiliation to her and her child. But today we look at this differently.

It's no longer inconvenient to return to diapers and few parents today want to be involved in toilet training their child for months on end. Your child won't be devastated, and in fact, most children who have accident after accident feel relief returning to diapers because the pressure is off. The child can relax, have more time to grow in the four important areas of developmental readiness, and then try again later.

Here's all you need to say, "You know, we've tried teaching you to use the toilet and you keep wetting and pooping in your underpants. I think we'll put your diapers back on and try again in a couple of months. Someday you'll go in the toilet, but for now I think it's time to go back to diapers."

If you do this, don't stop all the pre-toilet training activities you were doing before you introduced wearing underpants. Keep the potty chair in the bathroom. Put your child on the toilet twice a day and further, set your child on the toilet after each diaper change. Encourage your child to take stuffed animals and dolls to sit on the potty. You're not forgetting about educating your child to use the toilet just because you've returned to diapers. Your child isn't ready for underpants, but the toileting orientation process continues.

Stories from the Bathroom

❯ When Spencer turned two, Jane started steering him to use the toilet. When she noticed Spencer start to strain and grunt, she'd scoop him up, set him on the toilet, and he'd go without any problem. Soon Spencer was telling Mom when he needed to poop and off they'd go to the bathroom. He'd poop in his little potty chair and then empty the poop into the big toilet and flush. He really enjoyed this whole process.

Urinating was different; here they had no luck. Spencer simply was not interested. They had potty chairs in every room. Spencer put his Buddy doll on the potty chairs but he never tried to pee there. Mom tried everything. She threatened, "If you don't use the toilet, no TV." She tried rewards, "When you pee in the toilet, you'll get a candy."

Finally Mom consulted with Spencer's pediatrician. He said to return Spencer to diapers and wait. Spencer walked late at about 18 months. Because of the delay with walking, the doctor pointed out that this slow-down might affect Spencer's ability to learn to use the toilet too. So Mom took the doctor's advice and put Spencer in disposable training pants so he could get them up and down easily for bowel movements, yet have the diaper protection he needed.

The summer Spencer turned three Mom set out to train him again. She was a college student and had the summer off; it was the ideal time to train.

That summer it all seemed to come together for Spencer. Mom dressed him in easy-to-remove clothes, including underpants. She asked him frequently, "Do you need to pee?" Every time she used the toilet herself she took Spencer with her.

Mom was a single parent with one older daughter, so Spencer had no male role model around the house on a daily basis. But when Dad or Grandpa did come for a visit, she asked them to take Spencer with them to the bathroom so he could watch and try for himself.

At first Spencer had up to seven accidents a day, but gradually he made progress. Just after Spencer turned three on August fifth, he started to tell Mom, "I need to pee."

When Mom returned to college at the end of September, Spencer was doing fairly well, but still needed reminders and was having occasional accidents. Mom would run to the child care center between classes to take Spencer to the toilet. She worried that in this busy, stimulating center, Spencer would forget about urinating in the toilet. After a month she no longer needed to stop at the center between classes; Spencer was remembering about peeing and telling the child care providers when he had the urge to go.

At five and a half Spencer continued to wet his bed at night. The doctor reassured Mom that for Spencer this wasn't surprising; in time he would train through the night, but there was little she could do to speed the process.

Jane's approach in the above story was admirable. She combined patience, determination, and sensitivity to reach the desired goal. Jane and Spencer had a tougher and longer training period than most do, but more importantly, the child learned to use the toilet in the way that was right for him.

REGRESSION

Regression occurs when a child appears trained for two weeks or more and then reverts to having accident after accident. It also takes place as a result of stress after training is accomplished.

It's commonplace for children under two years old, or those who are slightly over two, to appear trained but were really not ready in the beginning. They want to please their parents so they work hard and really concentrate on not wetting or soiling their underpants. Soon they discover the toileting business is too much work; it requires too much time and concentration so they start having accidents.

If this is the case with your child, don't panic. Just get out those diapers again and realize it's temporary. Your child just needs a little more time to mature.

Stories from the Bathroom

❧ At two and a half Kyra appeared trained; for two weeks she had no accidents. Then she had a few wetting incidents. Mom didn't scold her, but was very disappointed when Kyra wet her underpants. Then Mom noticed some changes in Kyra's behavior. She stopped playing spontaneously; she just sat quietly on the floor looking worried and occupied about when it might be time to pee in the toilet. Mom sensed the stress Kyra was experiencing from trying to stay dry and put her back in diapers.

Kyra continued to poop in the toilet, but it wasn't until her third birthday that Mom put her back in panties. She trained very quickly on this second try.

Another factor to consider before introducing toilet training, or when the process stalls, is your family's stress level. Take a careful look at your home atmosphere. Is there a new baby in the house—or one imminent? Has Grandpa just moved in for three months? Are you getting ready to move across the street or across the country? Are you in the process of getting a divorce? Is your child starting or changing child care situations?

Any of these factors, and more, add stress to your life and your child's life and can hinder your child's ability to learn to use the toilet. Most families live with some stress daily, but if there's any new glaring change that is going to take time and adjustment for you or your child, wait until life calms down before jumping into toileting education.

If a child is eager to train, even if a new sibling is due to arrive soon, go ahead and train. The child can learn to use the toilet, but expect some regression when the baby actually arrives. The re-learning process goes quickly and the window of opportunity for learning hasn't slipped by.

Guiding your child takes concentration, persistence, and patience on your part. If you're adjusting to a new job or your spouse has just been laid off, wait. Starting the toileting process now might set your child up for failure; and you may be just setting yourself up for frustration.

Too many changes imposed on children at once usually hinders their success. Going from diapers to underpants and learning to control the bowel and bladder muscles is a necessary frustration children endure. But if this learning process is forced on top of other stresses, children may become too anxious to succeed.

Any stress can cause regression. If your child is trained and then begins having accidents, look at what is happening in your child's immediate environment that might be stressful.

Stories from the Bathroom

❭ Jamie was completely trained one month before her new baby sister arrived. Louise was reluctant to train her, but Jamie was interested, willing, and completely ready. It was a snap. When the new baby arrived on the scene, Jamie accepted this intrusion willingly at first. Then, after a few days, she asked, "When is that baby going back to the hospital?" Mom explained that baby Stephanie would not be going back to the hospital, that she was a member of the family now and would be living with them forever. Once this realization sunk in, Jamie started wetting her underpants two or three times a day.

This is not what Mom needed: a new baby and an almost three year old who wet the carpet, couch, or floor twice a day. Louise was horrified. She pleaded with Jamie to use the toilet, asked her why she was doing this, and told her only babies wet—not big girls like Jamie. With each accident Mom scolded Jamie and put her in her bedroom. The accidents started to escalate.

Finally, Louise consulted a child development specialist. Her advice was to put Jamie back in diapers. This new baby in the family added stress to Jamie's life and she responded by wetting her pants. She encouraged Louise to look at the situation from Jamie's perspective. When her baby sister was born, Jamie lost some of the positive attention she was accustomed to getting from Louise. Jamie discovered that wetting her pants got her the quick attention—even though negative—she was craving from her mom. Louise's emotional response contributed to more persistent wetting.

It took about a month of being back in diapers before Jamie decided on her own to return to panties. During this time Jamie had adjusted somewhat to life with her new baby sister.

The stress factor contributes to toileting regression. If your child regresses due to a new stress on the family, matter-of-factly clean up the accidents—have your child assist with the clean up as much as he is able—without scolding or shaming him. Don't call too much negative attention to the problem or get hysterical or disgusted. If your child's regression causes you to become emotional and out-of-control, this only compounds the problem.

It can be downright interesting—even exciting—for children to see parents hysterical; few can resist provoking you by peeing on the floor to get that emotional response.

For this reason, it's important if your child starts having accidents that your response be low key. You need to spend your energy on pinpointing the source of the stress. Decide what you can or can't do to relieve the stress. Time is often the best remedy; consider putting your child in disposable training pants or diapers until the stress is over and then go through the teaching process again. Don't panic; most likely the second try will be almost effortless.

Regression may also be the result of a medical problem. If your child has persistent setbacks it's always a good idea to consult with your physician.

CAN I HAVE A DIAPER, PLEASE?

Another common occurrence is for a child to be completely urine-trained, but to ask for a diaper when it's time to poop. This is what happened with Elizabeth in the story below.

Stories from the Bathroom

❥ Mom couldn't believe it. Here was her two-and-a-half-year-old child wearing pretty new panties, going into the bathroom on her own to urinate, but insisting on a diaper when it was time to poop. How could this be? And why?

Mom complied with her child's request for a diaper. Elizabeth had managed urine training almost totally on her own, so Mom decided to trust her need for a diaper for bowel movements. Two weeks passed before, all on her own, Elizabeth started pooping into the toilet.

Remember, urine training and bowel training are two separate processes. Often children learn one procedure before the other. Occasionally training occurs concurrently, but many children respond as Elizabeth did, insisting on a diaper when it's time to poop. If your child is asking for a diaper for bowel movements, go ahead and provide the diaper; refusing it may lead to bowel retention or a power struggle.

FEARS

Some children fear that if their stool falls into the toilet, everything else inside them will drop out as well. Remember, children's thinking is limited by their development; they can't yet reason the way adults do. When children get this frightening notion in their heads it's difficult to talk them out of it. Use empathy first, "I know you're scared to use the toilet. Pooping seems scary to you." Now explain, "When you use the toilet only poop and pee fall out of your body." If your child is afraid he'll be flushed away, validate the fear but reassure your child, "Only pee, poop, and toilet paper flush down the toilet, not people."

Stories from the Bathroom

❥ Linda placed a potty chair in the bathroom for 16-month-old Kevin to sit on. He would sit on it when his older sister used the large toilet. Then, for no apparent reason, he started to avoid the potty chair altogether. Mom thought he was afraid of his poop dropping out of him and into the toilet. Kevin coped with his fears by avoiding the toilet altogether.

According to Linda, Kevin had always been a difficult child to manage; she described him as "headstrong." He couldn't be pushed or even nudged when it came to dressing himself or cleaning up toys. Toileting instruction was no different; she met with lots of resistance from Kevin.

Kevin was also fastidious about cleanliness. He never used paint, hardly touched play dough, and didn't like to touch gooey foods. He was equally disgusted with poop and pee. He was an orderly child, lining up cars and toys neatly in rows and organizing his bedroom beyond what seemed typical for a young child.

Kevin protested each of Linda's attempts to train him. It was clear he had absolutely no interest in using the toilet. So when his third birthday approached, Mom enrolled him in a preschool that didn't require children be toilet trained.

At preschool Kevin was impressed by a friend's underwear. Although he couldn't quite bring himself to wear underwear, he consented to wear training diapers. After one bowel accident, Kevin started pooping in the toilet. At three and a half, he still wore the training diapers because he refused to pee in the toilet.

Linda knew from Kevin's temperament that if she made even a slight hint about using the toilet, it would cause an obstinate setback in his progress. She realized that he was proceeding in baby steps and was prompted only by his own interest and desire.

Even though Kevin was bowel trained, he wouldn't use strange toilets. He was also soaked each morning, but Linda didn't push nighttime dryness at all. Kevin wouldn't wear underpants and wouldn't even have them in his dresser drawer. Linda knew that someday he would wear underpants, but when this happened, it would be totally up to him and no one else.

Linda had no trouble teaching her older daughter to use the toilet. Kevin's reluctance to use the toilet caught her totally off guard. She soon discovered success occurred only when she completely dropped out of the picture. Her role became that of an interested, supportive observer.

Toilet training troubles and fears are varied and complex. The solution to many of these problems is a temporary return to diapers and a one-to-three month wait before resuming training. If you feel your frustration level rising and you're unable to discover a solution on your own, consult your pediatrician, a child development specialist, or a parent educator for ideas and help.

5

TO REWARD OR NOT TO REWARD:
THAT'S THE POTTY TRAINING QUESTION

Sean sits on the potty holding his Ernie doll. Dad smiles with approval and says, "Helen, look at Sean, he's sitting on the potty." Chelsey pees in the toilet, Mom gives her a sticker; when she poops, she's awarded a lollipop. Debbie announces to Sally's older brother and sister that Sally just pooped for the first time in the little potty chair they once used. They run to the bathroom to see. These situations are all examples of rewards that encourage children to learn to use the toilet.

Smiles, hugs, applause, and positive statements such as "Good for you, you're sitting on your little toilet while Mom sits on the big toilet," are social rewards. Candy, trinkets, or stickers for toileting results are tangible rewards. Social rewards are necessary for training all children. Tangible rewards can be used effectively to accomplish the toileting task, but they are not essential for every child.

SOCIAL REWARDS

Think about the positive attention you focused on your child as he learned to walk. It is so exciting to watch a child take those first brave steps and eventually toddle across the room. You automatically focus positive attention on your child as he makes any minor advancement toward confident walking. When he falls, you don't scold, you just wait and watch until he's ready to try again. When he does try again, you naturally turn, watch, smile, clap, and focus on him as he works to perfect this skill.

When you watch your child walk for the first time at thirteen months, you don't think about little Sara down the street who walked at nine months. When a child walks, it's the time that's right for him and that's all that's important.

As your toddler shows off this new skill, you're proud of him, but you know the accomplishment is his alone. You provided an environment that supports walking: a sturdy floor and a safe place to practice. You also provided emotional and social support, that is, positive attention and encouragement.

As he becomes an accomplished walker, you no longer need to cheer every step he takes around the house. The same forms of social rewards used for walking can be adapted when guiding your child to use the toilet.

Children need positive attention focused on each baby step they make toward success. Educating your child to use the toilet is a bit more complicated than attending to him as he learns to walk. With walking, you know to just wait and watch, and it will happen. In toilet instruction your role is to prompt and encourage your child as she makes the transition from diapers to underpants. You need to watch and show interest with no expectation for immediate success. Your child also needs you to suggest—and sometimes sensitively impose—the next step to toileting success. In toileting your role is trickier, but the positive reinforcement you provide is the same.

Positive Responses that Encourage Toileting Success:

- Watching your child with an adoring look as he sits on the toilet.

- Saying, "Good for you, you peed in the toilet."

- Describing, "You're grunting, you're trying to push out a poop into the toilet. Way to go."

- Responding, "I'll bet you're proud of yourself. You peed in your potty chair."

- Noticing, "I saw your Teddy bear sitting on the toilet. He likes to sit there."

- Reading your child a book as she sits on her little potty or on the big toilet.

- Clapping briefly after your child performs on the toilet.

- Calling Dad or Grandma on the phone and telling them about any toileting success; encouraging your child to make the call or letting your child overhear your conversation.

- Showing pride and establishing eye contact as your child sits on the toilet. Stating, "You pooped and peed in the toilet. You look proud and happy. Mom and Dad are proud and happy too."

- Bending down and talking to your child as he sits on his potty chair and practices.

POSITIVE—NOT NEGATIVE—REINFORCEMENT

If you give children attention for their positive actions, they continue to behave positively. If you pay too much attention to misbehavior, you'll see children continuing to behave negatively. Negative attention includes trying to talk children out of their unwanted or inappropriate behavior.

If your child refuses to sit on the toilet don't ask, "Why won't you sit on the potty?" and don't go on and on about the importance of learning the task. Parents often over-explain toileting procedures as if thinking the child will eventually say, "I get it. No problem, I'll poop in the toilet since you explained it so well." These attempts to convince your child draw too much negative attention to the topic and seldom influence behavior positively.

Instead, just say, "I know you don't want to practice, but you need to sit on the toilet for thirty seconds." Proceed, being firm and kind, but clear about what you expect. Then praise any effort made. "You tried, good for you."

Coercive tactics—"What will Grandma think when she comes to visit next week and you're not peeing in the toilet?"—are meaningless and confusing to a child and will hinder toileting success. Negative comments and rhetorical questions—"You peed your pants again? When are you going to grow up?"—serve no purpose either.

If children get positive attention for toileting attempts and successes, they usually progress in a timely way, correct for their developing bodies. If they get negative reinforcement for toileting accidents, or if you give them negative attention for not progressing on your preferred schedule, it will most likely hinder their progress. There's no need for negative comments or body language that communicates unhappiness or disgust.

Negative Responses that Hinder Toileting Success:

- Scolding, "You're too old and too big to be wearing diapers."

- Comparing, "Your friend Billy wears underpants and he's younger than you."
- Negatively reinforcing, "Another accident? Why do you keep doing this?"
- Labeling, "Big girls don't wear diapers—are you going to be a baby your whole life?"
- Looking disgusted or disapproving when your child isn't progressing as you expect.
- Scowling, establishing eye contact, shaking your head, and saying, "You make me so angry. I don't like you when you poop in your underpants."
- Screaming, "All your friends are trained, what's wrong with you?"

Parenting would be so easy if such negative comments changed children's behavior for the better. Unfortunately, this is rarely the case. Usually, disapproving statements leave children paralyzed and not knowing how to change their behavior. Since they don't know *what* to do, or how to do it, they simply keep on behaving in the same old negative fashion.

COMMUNICATING CLEARLY

There will be times when it is appropriate for you to let your child know how you feel and what you expect. Try this method: 1) Use the pronoun "I", 2) explain how you feel, 3) precisely describe the behavior you approve of or disapprove of, and 4) then tell your child what you expect.

Examples:

- "I'm angry. I don't want you to pee in your brother's baseball cap. You need to pee in the toilet."

- "I'm so proud of you! You pooped in the toilet. I'll bet you'll do it again tomorrow."
- "I'm tired of changing dirty diapers. I hope you learn to poop in the toilet soon."
- "I'm so happy you're wearing your pretty new underwear. Remember you're not supposed to pee or poop in them."
- "I'm disappointed you wet your underwear at preschool today. Please try to remember to use the toilet."

Positive comments are most effective when helping your child succeed. Negative responses usually work against improving toileting procedures and can harm your child's emotional well-being. When your child does have an accident or setback, it's usually most effective to matter-of-factly clean your child up. There is no need to establish eye contact or talk. Just clean the child and then evaluate your child's readiness for training. Do you continue with your plan? Do you change the plan? Do you put your child back in diapers?

Always remember, ultimate control lies with the child. It's her body and she's in control. You have lots of influence but it only goes so far. Your best tools are positive social rewards for each baby step your child makes toward learning to use the toilet.

DIAPER DAYS

Diaper changing time is usually a positive time for a parent and child. You make eye contact, talk, and laugh. One-on-one positive attention is focused totally on the child. Parents need to continue this same level of focus and positive attention as the child works toward being educated to use the toilet.

Stories from the Bathroom

❭ Diaper changing had always been a fun time for Sally and her son Braden. Sally would tell silly stories as she changed Braden's diapers. Then, with toilet instruction, this special time dropped out of sight. Braden seemed ready intellectually and physically, but he wasn't making much progress.

Suddenly a light went on for Sally. She enticed Braden to use the toilet with the promise of hearing one of the silly stories she told him when she changed his diapers. This was the key. She stopped the stories for diaper changes but told them when he practiced or performed on the toilet.

Braden had missed the stories and the attention they brought from Mom. When the stories and attention resumed while Braden sat on the toilet, he made progress quickly.

The point is obvious. Give your child the same amount of attention for toileting as you did for diaper changing and success will occur in a more timely fashion.

TANGIBLE REWARDS

It's common practice for parents today to reward children with candy or small toys when they urinate or have a bowel movement in the toilet.

Warning: If a child is not physically developed to the point where he can hold in his urine or stool and then release it into the toilet, a tangible reward system will not work and it is not fair to use this tactic on the child. You would be expecting a child to do something for which he lacks the physical maturity. So be certain if you try rewarding a child with trinkets that he's developed enough physically to accomplish the task.

Sometimes a reward system helps and sometimes it backfires, complicating the toileting process. For example, Alex, in the story below, was not interested in any reward offered by Mom or Dad.

Stories from the Bathroom

❭ Alex was a child determined to train himself in his very own way and time. One day Mom suggested to Alex that she'd buy him the Lego® set he really wanted if he'd wear underwear for just one hour on one day. She secretly thought that if he only tried wearing underwear once he'd realize they weren't so bad after all, and he might just start wearing them full time. No way. Alex refused the offer.

Some children respond positively to such tangible rewards. A trinket for success helps get them over the hump of "going" in diapers to "going" in the toilet. It depersonalizes the process and offers the child a choice. The child is not using the toilet to please Mom or Dad, he's using it to get the reward. Whenever children have a choice in a situation it gives them power and control. Here's an example of how a reward system provided just that feeling of control.

Stories from the Bathroom

❭ Three-year-old Jeremy loved the colorful little plastic cars that were displayed in large jars at the drug store where his mom shopped. He always begged for one.

Jeremy was having a little trouble with training. A power struggle was starting to build between him and his mother. Mom would ask Jeremy to sit on the toilet but usually he'd refuse by stomping his foot and yelling, "No, no!" Then Mom told Jeremy he couldn't watch TV until he tried to pee or poop on the toilet. Jeremy didn't care, he just sat on the floor and played with his cars and usually wet or pooped his pants.

Mom knew Jeremy was socially, intellectually, and physically ready, but for some reason she couldn't get him to go in the toilet. There was a push–pull going on between the two that both could feel. So Mom tried a reward system.

She said, "Jeremy, I bought a jar of these plastic cars at the drug store today. You have a choice: You can go in the toilet and get one of these plastic cars, or you can choose to pee in your underwear. It's fine with me if you go in your underwear, but when you do, you won't get one of these cars."

Jeremy was dry for up to two hours so Mom knew he had control. When Jeremy went in his underwear rather than in the toilet, all Mom said was, "Jeremy you went in your underwear. Remember, when you go in the toilet you'll get one of these." She pointed to the jar full of plastic cars displayed in the bathroom. When Jeremy did go in the toilet, he picked a car from the jar.

After two or three days, Jeremy was doing great. He was dry most of the day and had collected several cars. He became so skilled, he could stop and start peeing with amazing control. So he tried this: He peed a little into the toilet and chose a car from the jar. Fifteen minutes later he was back in the bathroom going a little more for another car. Mom caught on quickly to his scheme. She said, "Jeremy you must empty your bladder to get a car. I'll watch you pee to see if you've completely emptied your bladder."

Once the colorful plastic cars in the jar were gone, the reward system was over. Did Jeremy start peeing his pants again? Not at all. Jeremy was accustomed to having dry pants. The reward system helped Jeremy make the transition from peeing and pooping in his underwear to doing so in the toilet. There was no need to buy more cars, or to raise the ante with more enticing rewards.

A reward must be immediate. The child must get the trinket as soon as she performs. A plan that requires a child to stay dry and clean for a week before getting the reward won't work. A week is too long in the life of a child. It's best to give a little reward each time the child pees or poops into the toilet.

If you want to give a more substantial reward than a trinket, then you can use a chart and sticker system. The child earns a star or sticker every time she performs in the toilet. Once she earns ten stickers, she gets the toy. Remember, it is not fair to remove stickers for accidents.

Another factor important for successful use of rewards is this: The reward must be something the child *really* wants. If you try to motivate a child with stickers when what she really loves are marshmallows, you're wasting your time.

Stories from the Bathroom

❦ Sloane, at two years, nine months, was negative about everything—which is typical for a child her age. Above all, she cut a wide swath around the potty chair in the bathroom. She avoided it at all costs.

Her mom, Helen, knew Sloane had bladder control because she woke up dry every morning. Once Helen gently placed her on her potty chair. The result: a thirty minute temper tantrum. Afterwards Sloane wouldn't even enter the bathroom except when Helen carried her in there for her bath.

Helen noticed that Sloane loved pennies. She had five and played with them everyday. She would put them in one purse, carry them around for a while, then transfer the coins to another purse.

One day Sloane asked her mother for another penny. Opportunity knocked. Helen said, "You can have a penny, but you must sit on your little potty chair first." It worked.

Sloane ran to the bathroom and sat for a few seconds on her potty chair with her purse and pennies in hand. She was not required to perform; she did not even have to take off her diaper. Helen awarded Sloane her penny, which she added to her collection.

Helen and Sloane continued this routine all day. Sloane collected about ten more pennies. The next day Helen told her she could get a penny only if she sat on the potty while Mom read her a short story. Sloane collected five more pennies that day.

The following day, Helen told Sloane she could have ten pennies if she'd wear panties. Sloane agreed. That morning she sat on the potty and peed as Helen read her a story. Sloane was on her way to being trained.

The next day Helen went to the bank to obtain a roll of brand new pennies. She showed the pennies to Sloane, who was dazzled by their newness and sparkle. Helen simply explained, "Sloane, today and from now on you will receive a penny when you pee or poop in your potty chair." Sloane did have a few accidents, but the penny plan was tremendously effective. Soon, she was completely trained. Helen continued to offer the pennies with each success in the toilet until the pennies ran out.

Two year olds, with their negative attitudes, are often resistant to using the toilet at first, because it means compliance. Compliance symbolizes dependency, and two year olds are pushing for independence and exercising their own control. Sloane, in the example above, worked for pennies, which put her in control of the process.

Social rewards are essential to toilet training children. Tangible rewards can be very useful, but are not always necessary. Use your knowledge of your child to decide whether to use tangible rewards to motivate training.

6

UNPLUGGING POWER STRUGGLES

Parents and children get into power struggles over a wide variety of issues. There's the getting dressed power struggle, the car seat power struggle, and the daily battle over getting out the door on time, just to name a few. A power struggle is an emotional battle between parent and child over who is in control. When such a power play ends, usually nothing is resolved and the same battle occurs again and again.

Potty training power struggles occur when parents make too much of an emotional investment in educating their child to use the toilet. For successful guidance, parents need a clear idea of where their influence begins and ends. Keep in mind your child is a separate individual and ultimate control lies with him. You can put your children in bed, but you can't control when they actually fall asleep. You can provide nutritious and tasty food, but you can't make them swallow it.

Likewise, you can entice and encourage children to use the toilet, but your influence is limited. Parents who cross the line to forceful and emotional tactics often end up in power struggles—which are emotional tug-of-wars over control. Parents who are prone to such power plays generally have trouble seeing their child as a separate person; they believe they can exert control over the child's bowel and bladder habits. The child knows that he and he alone controls this process, digs in his heels, and refuses to comply with his parents' demands.

Stories from the Bathroom

❢ James was 33 months old when his parents, Jerry and Julie, started training him. He learned to urinate in the toilet quickly and easily. Bowel movements were a different story. He had a tendency toward constipation, so his bowel movements occasionally caused some pain.

Jerry and Julie tried every technique possible to entice James to use the toilet. Frst, they tried rewards: a new toy car if he pooped into the toilet. Then, punishments: a ten-minute time out in his bedroom every time he pooped his pants. No matter what, he continued to poop in his underwear. Every week for nine months Jerry and Julie introduced different methods. They would start each technique with a calm and cool demeanor which soon deteriorated into strong expressions of anger and exasperation. James always ended up in tears.

Their last approach was to watch James intently all day long, watching for the first strain or grunt that indicated the start of a bowel movement. When they sensed he was on the verge of pushing out a poop, they'd scoop him up and set him on the toilet. As he sat on the toilet they would encourage him to go. He would sit there for the longest time, refusing to poop into the toilet. As soon as he got off, he filled his pants. His control was remarkable.

When James did this, his parents flew into emotional pleas for change. "You pooped in your pants again? Why do you keep doing this? It's such a mess. You're too big for this. It's disgusting. I can't stand cleaning up these dirty pants any longer."

It's easy to see that emotions run high in power struggles. But it was just that emotional response from Jerry and Julie that kept the power struggle going. Very likely, this is what was happening: On some level, James realized that pooping in his pants was all it took for his parents to fly into a rage. He simply couldn't resist controlling his parents' emotional states and the personal sense of power this brought him.

On the surface an angry parental stance might appear a viable technique to promote toilet training. After all, don't children want to please their parents and avoid angry outbursts? Maybe some children do, but not all.

The family's negative routine compounded the problem. It went like this: Mom and Dad would develop a new plan to persuade James to poop in the toilet. No matter what, he refused to comply, and pooped his pants. Mom and Dad became mad and frustrated and James was reduced to tears. Then, Mom and Dad shrugged their shoulders and threw up their hands. Lastly, one parent cleaned him up, all the while pleading with him and trying to convince him of the importance of pooping in the toilet. This routine—even though unpleasant—brought consistency to James' day.

Children continually pull their parents back into old ways of behaving—even negative ways—because those routines made life predictable. Changing such a routine is difficult, but not impossible.

Remember, a key factor contributing to the problem in the example above is that James received lots of attention for the negative bowel movement routine. Too much of the relationship existing between James and his parents revolved around his bowel habits. To end the battle, his parents would need to change the focus of their relationship with their son.

RESPONDING TO POWER STRUGGLES

To end a power struggle parents need a plan and a matter-of-fact attitude. Sometimes parents resolve such a struggle by holding onto their power and control; this is essential when the issue concerns a child's safety—such as wearing a seat belt. In other situations, agreement between parent and child can be reached by offering the child a choice. For example, if Dad is battling with his daughter over getting dressed, offering her a choice about what to wear often resolves the problem. Choices provide children with a measure of control and often defuse a power struggle.

In some situations, such as potty training, it's appropriate for a parent to drop out of the power struggle. When parents try to exert control in an area where they have no control, like bowel and bladder habits, their best option is to drop out. Parents have lots of influence when it comes to teaching their child to use the toilet, but if the learning process ends and an emotional battle erupts, parents must drop back. Julie and Jerry from the example above, unfortunately, didn't do this. They believed they could eventually convince their son to poop in the toilet. They thought they could figure out a technique to control what was going on inside his body.

They made endless attempts to convince James to cooperate. They would talk and talk to James about the importance of using the toilet and about how easy life would be if only he would change his bowel habits. They would ask him why he kept pooping his pants? They would even ask him how he planned to go through life if he never pooped in the toilet?

Like many parents, they somehow believed they'd be able to get across to their son how easy and important it is to go in the toilet, and he should agree and cooperate. An outcome like this is highly unlikely.

To end such a contest of wills, parents need to admit they have lost the battle. When they come to this realization they must drop out of the conflict and turn control completely over to their child. It is paradoxical, but when parents let go of their involvement, the child is likely to begin to use the toilet.

STEPS TO END A POTTY TRAINING POWER STRUGGLE

Sometimes problems between parent and child involve bowel training, sometimes urine training, and sometimes both. Whatever the extent of the problem, the remedy is similar. The following is a bowel training example, but you can easily adapt the approach to a urine training struggle as well.

Step One

Say this to your child, "You don't have to poop in the toilet if you don't want to. Someday you will poop in the toilet, but for now it's okay with me if you continue to poop in your underwear. The decision to poop in the toilet is completely under your control. I can't force you."

Step Two

When the child poops his pants take him to the bathroom and clean him up. It's important to be totally matter–of–fact in your body language and voice inflection. Do not sigh, look disgusted, annoyed, or angry. Try not to establish eye contact as you clean your child; don't talk, just clean him up as quickly as possible and then move on through the day.

Step Three

Do not look for signs of when your child is about to poop. In fact, if you notice he is pooping his pants, slowly walk away. You don't want to give your child any attention when he is pooping in his underwear. Don't talk about bowel training in front of him. Don't hint or make any suggestions about using the toilet.

Step Four

Establish a relationship with your child totally separate from bowel training. (See Chapter 9 for suggestions.)

Step Five

After a week or so of this new approach, inform your child that you can no longer clean him up after he has a bowel movement in his underwear. When the child poops in his pants, escort him to the bathroom and put him in the bathtub. Coach him through each step of the clean up, being completely nonchalant in your body language and voice inflection. You need to encourage him, being friendly and kind, but it's important to remain firm about him cleaning *himself* up as much as he is able. In the end, it's important for you to check that he is clean, and, if necessary, finish up the final wipes yourself.

Your goal is to teach your child the natural consequence for pooping in his pants is cleaning himself up. It's okay if your child expresses some frustration here, but be careful not to send the message that this is a punishment.

Step Six

If the child gets emotional, empathize, "I know it's hard work cleaning yourself after you poop your pants. It's a mess. You don't like doing it." Then set the limit again, "Nevertheless, when you poop in your underwear it's your job to wash yourself. I'll help get your shoes and socks off." You may be tempted to say, "If you'd poop in the toilet you wouldn't have this mess to deal with." But it's best not to make this comment. Instead, try an up-beat approach, "Someday you'll poop in the toilet. Then you won't need to clean yourself up."

Step Seven

It's a good idea to invite a young cousin, neighbor, or friend over to play who is skilled in using the toilet. Be sure to ask the parents if your child can go in the bathroom with their child so your child can see how the other child manages pooping in the toilet. Also, ask your young visitor for permission. Be careful how involved you get in staging this event. The more naturally the event occurs, the better.

Another option is to put your child in a quality child care setting a couple of days a week so he can see the ease with which other children poop in the toilet. Watching children in this new environment, with trained teachers to help, might inspire your child to use the toilet for pooping too. Having other children around to demonstrate puts the activity in your child's realm of possibility.

The goal is for your child to discover that pooping in the toilet is much easier than cleaning up messy underpants. Realize that this is something your child must learn in his own way and time.

Step Eight

Set two times daily when your child is required to sit on the toilet. You can call it Poo–Poo Time. Assure your child he is not required to perform, he only needs to sit on the toilet for five minutes. In the beginning, he might sit there only a minute or so; but slowly increase the time to five minutes. You can read him a story, he can look at books himself, or he can listen to a story on a tape recorder.

At first he can sit on the toilet with his clothes on, but later encourage him to pull his pants down. Poo-Poo Time helps the child become comfortable with sitting on the toilet. Then when the time is right for him to use it, the experience won't be foreign or scary.

Step Nine

Now you must step back emotionally and calmly wait until your child finally decides for himself to poop in the toilet. You can't hurry the process.

Step Ten

When your child finally does go in the toilet, show interest, but don't go overboard with praise. A simple "Good for you" is all that's necessary, along with a homemade certificate of "Congratulations" to post on the refrigerator.

Here's a detailed story of how one mom solved a potty training power struggle.

Stories from the Bathroom

❧ Amy was almost five and would be attending kindergarten in the fall. She was bowel trained but still peed her pants two or three times a day. When her mom, Rebecca, picked her up from preschool, Amy would be involved in play and totally wet; she didn't seem to notice or be bothered by her soaked clothes.

As Rebecca tried to solve this urinating puzzle, she changed tactics almost daily. One day she'd try rewarding Amy with a new toy for peeing in the toilet, but when Amy had an accident she'd lose control emotionally and yell or reprimand rather than just asking Amy to put on clean clothes. The next day she tried to completely ignore the wet pants, but by the second accident she found herself tense and angry. The following day Rebecca would remind Amy hourly to sit on the toilet. Amy would sit there. Sometimes she'd pee and sometimes she wouldn't, but she continued to have accidents. Changing approaches daily was very confusing for Amy.

Rebecca was panicked and engaged in a power struggle with Amy. She knew she shouldn't scold, yell, and punish, but she felt her emotions escalating when it came to Amy's wetting. She wondered what would happen next year in kindergarten if she peed her pants there? What if wetting her pants continued into the first grade?

Rebecca claimed what exasperated her most was that the wet pants didn't seem to bother Amy at all. She thought if she could see Amy upset about soaked panties, or at least trying to make it to the toilet, she could be more patient. But Amy did not appear to be upset.

Rebecca decided to consult Amy's pediatrician. The doctor surmised that Amy received little sensation from her bladder about the need to go. Some children feel this sensation vividly, but not Amy. The result was that she required more maturing time than most children to read the signal from her body about knowing when it was time to pee.

Amy's disinterest frustrated Rebecca, but she realized there was no way for her to control Amy's response to the wetting situation. Rebecca could control her own emotional reaction, but she couldn't control her daughter's. Besides, it was possible since her mom was so upset and concerned about the wetting, Amy felt she didn't need to be.

The pediatrician recommended Rebecca set aside her emotions and develop a plan. She needed to stick with it as long as necessary for Amy's urinating behavior to improve.

More factors contributed to the problem: Rebecca was worried how friends and family were judging Amy. She saw the raised eyebrows and head shaking from those around her. Also, Dad wanted to spank Amy each time she peed her pants. He was convinced if Amy knew she'd get a spanking, she'd start using the toilet to avoid the punishment. He didn't want to believe what the doctor said about the low sensation from her bladder.

The pediatrician advised Rebecca and her husband to view Amy's problem as a delay in development. If a specialist told them that Amy wouldn't be able to walk until some time between five and six years old, Rebecca wouldn't yell at her to just try to get up and cross the room. She would develop patience and explain the problem to family and friends; she would provide assistance and guidance as Amy struggled to learn to walk.

Rebecca had to adopt this same attitude as she helped Amy learn to read the signals from her body about the need to go. She had to explain the problem to those close to her and ask for their support. She had to make it clear to her husband that spanking would not motivate their daughter to pee in the toilet.*

---

*Spanking is never appropriate when guiding a child toward learning to use the toilet. In fact, swats on the bottom actually delay the process by humiliating the child and building up resentment between parent and child.

Rebecca had to consider the possibility that Amy might pee her pants in kindergarten and even into first grade. If this happened she planned to inform the teachers of the problem, keep extra clothes at school, and explain to Amy what to do when she was wet.

Rebecca also needed to explain the situation to her daughter. She said, "Amy, the doctor says your body is different than some children's. Many children feel the need to pee clearly; it's almost like a fire engine's siren telling them it's time to run to the bathroom and go in the toilet. Your body doesn't give out loud signals—your body gives out quiet signals, so you must listen harder. Sometimes you will hear it, sometimes you won't. After a while you'll hear it every single time."

Then Rebecca had to decide how she would proceed on a daily basis. She considered two possible methods.

▪ First option. Remind Amy to use the toilet every hour. Realize that sometimes she will urinate and sometimes she won't. Also realize she may still have accidents. The idea behind this method is to get Amy in the habit of thinking about the need to go, using the toilet, hopefully reading her body, and eventually gaining control. It also might provide more successes.

▪ Second option. Do nothing, except see that Amy change her clothes when wet. This approach puts the ball in Amy's court. Know and trust that in time, she will catch on all on her own.

Rebecca chose the second option, with one modification. At home, Amy seldom experienced urinating mishaps. At preschool, or when playing at friends' houses, the accidents occurred more often. Analyzing this aspect of the problem, Rebecca decided to put her in underwear with a light rubber pant to hold in the pee when she was away from home. This way she could avoid the negative attention from onlookers when her clothes were damp.

Once parents develop a plan to end a power struggle, it's important they stick with it. They need to wait about three weeks for significant improvement. Quick fixes seldom occur. Keep in mind the three P's: Persistence, Patience, and a Plan. Remember that changing daily from plan to plan is quite bewildering to children and hinders more than it helps.

AVOIDING A POWER STRUGGLE

Many children who are urine trained still request a diaper for their bowel movements. When this happens parents often feel controlled by their child and respond by refusing the diaper, pleading for performance on the toilet instead, or placing pressure on the child to switch from a diaper to the toilet. The end result is a power struggle. This problem is more common than you think, so there's no need to feel alone.

It's important to provide the diaper for your child. If you don't, many children (like John in the story below) will refuse to poop for days, starting on a path of constipation, bowel retention, and possibly encopresis (see Chapter 8 for more information). This is dangerous for a child's body.

If your child requests a diaper for bowel movements well after he or she is urine trained, try gradually guiding the child toward pooping in the toilet. Remember not to panic; your child *will* eventually poop there.

Stories from the Bathroom

❭ Lucy's son, Jon, was almost four years old. He insisted on wearing a diaper for his bowel movements. He had been urine trained for over a year, but would not poop in the toilet.

Lucy tried every trick in the book. She told him she'd take him to the toy store and buy him anything he wanted if he'd poop in the toilet just once. It did no good. She yelled, restricted, pleaded, reasoned, and even spanked, but nothing coerced him to perform on the toilet.

So, finally, when the box of diapers ran out, Lucy informed him that she was not going to buy any more. She thought that if he didn't have diapers he'd be forced to go in the toilet. Jon retained his bowel movement for five days.

Wisely, Lucy bought diapers again. Jon went back to the old, "I need a diaper," routine. Off he went to his bedroom to poop and then Lucy cleaned him up.

After giving it some thought, Lucy came up with the following plan. One day she said to her son, "Jon, it's your body. If you need a diaper the rest of your life, I will see that you have one and I will love you just the same.

"But once you get your diaper on, I'd like you to go into the bathroom for your bowel movement. That way you won't smell up your bedroom and it's easier for me to clean you up in there." Jon agreed.

After a few days of pooping in his diaper in the bathroom, Lucy requested, "Jon, now when I put a diaper on, I'd like you to sit on the toilet." At first, he had trouble pushing a poop out as he sat on the toilet with his diaper on. It was difficult to change positions from squatting to sitting. In time, with encouragement from his mom, he adjusted to sitting on the toilet with the diaper still in place.

Lucy also established a practice time when Jon was required to sit on the toilet twice a day with his underwear off for a brief amount of time, to rehearse pooping in the toilet. Lucy assured Jon he was not expected to go, he just needed to sit there.

As he sat on the toilet to practice, Lucy told him a made-up story about a little boy who didn't want to poop in the toilet. The story included parts about the boy practicing pooping on the toilet but ending up going in his diaper. The story ended with the boy deciding one day it would be just fine to go in the toilet and how proud the boy felt when he finally accomplished this task. Jon enjoyed the story. If Lucy left out or changed even one part he corrected her.

Finally one day, out of the blue, as Jon was sitting on the toilet with his diaper in place, he said, "You can take my diaper off, Mom," and that was the end of it. He pooped into the toilet. This process took two weeks.

So what's to be learned from the stories of James, Amy, and Jon? First, children are in control of their bowels and bladders. There is no way to force a child to go in the toilet. In fact, if you get into an emotional power struggle, children will often be delayed instead of progressing steadily on their own potty–learning timeline. Performing on the toilet must be your child's decision, not yours.

PERSONALITY TYPES PRONE TO POWER STRUGGLES

There seems to be a similarity among parents who engage in potty training power struggles with their children. The parent tends to be controlling in many aspects of parenting. They choose the child's clothes, activities, food, and friends and are often strict disciplinarians.

Parents who are prone to power struggles often insist on mature behavior long before the child is ready. They demand a child walk a narrow path of acceptable behavior and may punish harshly when the child strays from that path. The child unconsciously feels that the only thing in his life he can control are his bowels and bladder and goes overboard to prove this.

So check yourself out. Can you lighten up? Can you alter your expectations regarding your child's behavior? Try asking yourself each time you make a decision for your child, "Is this a decision my child could be making for himself?" If the answer is yes, back off and let him make it.

This will give your child control in positive and appropriate areas of his life, and it won't be as important for him to hold onto those bowel movements.

Stories from the Bathroom

❥ This was the case with Kathy, Brad, and their son Michael. A potty training power struggle was well underway. At age three Michael refused to poop in the toilet. His mom and dad would force him to sit on the toilet; they would hold him there because they knew he needed to empty his bowel. Instead of pooping in the toilet or messing his underwear, Michael began to retain his bowel movements for days. Kathy was a nurse and knew this was unhealthy for his body.

Michael would finally go when Mom or Dad would allow him to wear a diaper to poop, but this was only after angry demands to go in the toilet.

Both Brad and Kathy were enmeshed at a deep emotional level in the bowel training issue with Michael. They could not see Michael as a separate person who alone was in control of his bodily functions. They knew they needed to gain control of their emotions, but they just couldn't. Michael's bowel activity was dominating not only their relationship with their son but their relationship with each other. Red flags were flying all over the place.

Kathy called Michael's pediatrician who referred her to a psychologist specializing in play therapy. Once the sessions between Michael and the therapist began, the bowel issue relaxed for Kathy and Brad. Michael was getting the help he needed so they felt able to drop out of the power struggle. Within weeks Michael was pooping in the toilet.

If your child is resistant to all attempts to toilet train or if you feel your child is suffering emotionally or psychologically, consider getting a referral from your pediatrician or family practice physician to see a psychologist or psychiatrist specializing in children. Sometimes it takes a trained therapist to help a child overcome resistance to toileting. Also, you will feel relief when the burden of training is lifted from your shoulders to a skilled professional's.

TWO IMPORTANT POINTS

☑ When toileting problems occur, consult your child's pediatrician or your family doctor first. Have your child checked out physically to make sure all body parts are working correctly. If your child seems to lack bladder control, or if he holds his bowel movements in for more than five days, definitely see the doctor.

☑ Don't leave children in wet or poopy diapers or underwear. Although some parents believe if they prolong the yucky feeling of messy or wet the child will be motivated to use the toilet, it's more effective, humane and sanitary to change the child in a timely fashion so he becomes accustomed to dry and clean undergarments. It also avoids the rashes or yeast infections caused by unchanged diapers.

7

NIGHT TRAINING AND BED WETTING

After your child is confidently using the toilet during the day, it's time to think about encouraging her to stay dry for naps and nighttime. Often, naptime dryness happens naturally with very little prompting from parents. The bladder muscles develop enough strength to hold in urine when the child sleeps. Other children give up napping, so the problem disappears with the naps.

Some parents are reluctant to put a diaper on for naps or nighttime as they fear this gives the child a mixed message about using the toilet and using a diaper. If you've told the child, "No more diapers—only babies use diapers" then why does your big girl or boy need a diaper on for naps? You wonder, what does this say to the child?

First of all, you can avoid this bind by not equating babies with diapers. Many toddlers wear diapers; some three year olds wear diapers; people with bladder control problems wear diapers; and many older people wear diapers. Some children who use the toilet during the day need a diaper for their nap or through the night.

When your child is using the toilet confidently while awake and questions you as you're putting a diaper on for nap or bedtime, just reassure your child this way, "Someday you won't need a diaper when you're sleeping, but for now it's best to wear one so your clothes, pajamas, sheets, and blankets don't get wet."

Stories from the Bathroom

❩ Kristen, nearly three, had just learned to use the toilet. As Nancy, her mom, put a diaper on her for bed, Kristen protested, "I don't want a diaper, Mom." Nancy didn't want to face wet sheets in the morning or be wakened by Kristen in the middle of the night after wetting her bed. But Kristen insisted on pajamas only. Miraculously, Kristen woke up dry the next morning. Staying dry all day and all night happened quickly and easily for Kristen.

Many children like Kristen learn to stay dry at night while learning at the same time to use the toilet during the day. Other children gain nighttime control about six months after they regularly use the toilet during the day.

Stories from the Bathroom

❩ Grant learned to pee and poop in the toilet just after his third birthday, but each morning his diaper was soaked. After Grant turned three and a half his mom made this suggestion, "Grant, I want you to try sleeping through the night without a diaper." Grant agreed. It was amazing; the next morning Grant woke up dry. Why? When the diaper was in place it gave Grant the license to pee. Without the diaper, he was aware of the need to hold in his urine all through the night.

Even though Grant stayed dry most nights, he occasionally wet his bed until he turned eight years old. The wetting episodes occurred whenever there was a slight disruption in Grant's life: a vacation, a friend over to spend the night, staying at Grandma's, the start of school each year. For about a month after the beginning of kindergarten, first and second grade Grant's bed was wet most mornings. Mom caught on to Grant's pattern of stress-related nighttime wetting and was never shocked when it occurred. By third grade these temporary wetting episodes ended on their own.

STRESS

Many children respond to the stress of change in their lives by bed wetting. A new sibling, parents' divorce, death in the family, a new school, a relocation, or a long-term house guest are all stressful to children. If your child is dry through the night and suddenly starts wetting, consider that a sign of stress. Until the stress is relieved, or until the child has adjusted to it, the bed wetting will probably continue. Be understanding and don't panic—in time, your child will go back to dry nights.

Stories from the Bathroom

At five Cynthia was dry about three nights a week; the other four nights she wet her bed. Maryanne reminded Cynthia each night before bed to try to stay dry. On occasion she'd get Cynthia up during the night to urinate into the toilet; sometimes Cynthia would go, and sometimes she was too groggy to go. Either way, Cynthia continued to wet her bed several nights a week.

Maryanne decided to try an incentive program to help Cynthia control her bladder every night. She used a reward system. Maryanne placed a star chart on the back of

Cynthia's bedroom door. On the mornings she woke up dry, she received a star. After earning five stars, she could purchase a video to keep as her very own. If she had a nighttime accident, no stars were added and no stars were removed.

This was all the incentive Cynthia needed. After three weeks Cynthia trained herself to stay dry. Sometimes she'd wake herself up in the middle of the night to urinate into the toilet. The reward system helped her gain nighttime control.

There are four important factors to keep in mind when developing a star chart:

- The dry nights don't need to occur consecutively. If your child has three dry nights and then wets, it's not fair to take away a star the child has already earned. Subtracting stars is very discouraging; the child just might give up.

- Be certain to choose a reward you know will motivate your child to work toward the goal.

- Place the chart on the inside of your child's bedroom door. The successes and setbacks are between you and your child only; there is no need to involve the rest of the family.

- Don't make the reward too far in the future. You might start with three dry nights and then a reward. Then move the goal to six dry nights. This way your child builds on her successes and gains confidence at the same time. The expectation of ten dry nights before a reward will probably defeat the plan.

For Cynthia, in the example above, this plan was effective. Her body had developed to the point where she could hold in her urine all night—wetting the bed had only been a habit. The reward system provided the incentive to move from wet to dry nights.

If you try an incentive program and after three weeks you see your child makes little or no progress, end it. Some children don't gain control through the night so easily.

BED WETTING

Some children continue to wet the bed after their sixth birthday. If your child climbs out of bed each morning with wet pajamas and sheets, don't feel alone; 10% of all five year olds and 5% of ten year olds have the problem of bed wetting (nocturnal enuresis). Some children do not gain control until puberty. Bed wetting is most common in boys and it is often an inherited trait; usually children who have difficulty gaining control have a parent who had the same problem as a child.

Bed wetting after age six usually has a physical component. There are many reasons why a child might wet the bed: slow physical maturation, sound sleeping, physical abnormalities, and a deficiency in antidiuretic hormone (ADH—discussed in detail on page 90). Each of these physical components can be addressed with various techniques or treated by professionals.

However, some parents don't understand the physical and genetic causes and think if their child just tries harder he can manage to stay dry all night long. They may accuse the child of not caring or being lazy or believe their child is wetting the bed on purpose just to make them angry.

Stories from the Bathroom

❥ First thing each morning Susan would check nine-year-old Peter's bed for wetness. Her day would get off to a bad start if the bed was wet. She ranted and raved, "Why can't you just get up in the middle of the night and pee in the toilet? Don't you know I'm tired of all these wet sheets?

Your room stinks and your friends won't want to play at your house because of the smell in your room."

Peter just ignored his mom and this made her more exasperated. Susan was upset that Peter didn't show any signs of disappointment or frustration regarding his wet bed. She wondered if he even cared about trying to develop nighttime control.

Finally, Susan consulted a child development specialist. The specialist compared Peter's bed wetting to children who get nose bleeds in the middle of the night: they don't feel it, they just wake up with blood on their pillow and wonder how it happened. If the problem persists, the specialist explained, a child learns to wake up to take care of it, but usually the nose bleeds eventually end on their own. Bed wetting is not that different. The specialist further explained that when toilet training or bed wetting becomes more important to the parent than to the child, the child shuts down any natural desire to progress further.

A NEW ATTITUDE

In order to eventually achieve nighttime dryness, you must believe that, underneath it all, your child wants to stop wetting. Let go of the idea that your child is doing it just to irritate you. At the same time you need to accept the fact that your child's body just isn't developed enough to manage staying dry all night long.

Try hard to set your emotions aside. An angry or dispirited response from you will not change the situation. If you expect and even demand your child control bed wetting when he can't (because of physiological reasons) he feels ashamed of himself and his self-esteem is harmed.

It's important to notice how wetting the bed affects your child. Some children feel discouraged. They really try but the problem persists. Your child knows other kids don't wet the bed, so why does it happen to him?

It's important to explain to your child that bodies develop at different rates. Tell your child there is probably a delay in his physical maturation; the needed connection between his bladder and brain is just taking longer to develop. If your child is a sound sleeper, include this in your explanation. "You sleep so deeply, your brain doesn't get the message—or it ignores the message—that your bladder is full. Consequently, when your bladder is full, it simply empties by itself. Someday, when you're a little older, you'll wake up dry."

CONSULT YOUR PHYSICIAN

Since parents don't always know the reason for their child's bed wetting, it is advisable to consult your doctor on the matter. Occasionally, physical abnormalities in the urinary tract or persistent urinary infections cause bed-wetting.

ANTIDIURETIC HORMONE

If your child is past the age of six and continues to soak his bed each night, it's important to discuss with your doctor the possibility of a deficiency of arginine vasopressin, the antidiuretic hormone commonly referred to as ADH. Most people's bodies increase their production of ADH as they sleep, which limits the production of urine. Children who wet the bed may be deficient in their ability to produce the hormone and consequently have trouble holding their urine all night.

Administering ADH to your child just might be the answer for nighttime control. A synthetic equivalent of the antidiuretic hormone—desmopressin acetate—is usually administered by a nasal spray. There are possible side effects: headache, nasal stuffiness, and abdominal cramps.

Although these side effects are infrequent, it's important to discuss them with your doctor.

IS THERE ANYTHING THAT CAN BE DONE?

No matter what the physical source of the bed wetting problem, here are some things to try.

- When your child is home (not at school) encourage him to wait as long as possible when it's time to urinate. This technique stretches the bladder so it can hold more urine and it might help delay the need to urinate in the middle of the night.

- As your child is urinating, have him stop and start, stop and start. This strengthens the muscles that hold the urine in.

- Any teasing from siblings needs to be stopped. Here's all you need to say, "Sam wets the bed just like I did when I was a child. Someday he'll stay dry at night, but right now he can't help himself. Teasing only makes Sam feel bad. He needs your understanding. I will not allow you to tease him."

- Turn the responsibility for the wet bed over to your child. One girl was seven before gaining nighttime control. Between ages five and six she slept in a slumber bag; this simplified the laundry and bed changing process. It was her responsibility to put her slumber bag in the wash each morning. She also added the soap and started the machine.

It's common for parents to try getting their child up before they themselves go to bed each night to pee in the toilet. They believe it will train the child to wake himself up. This approach has limited success. Some nights the child will urinate, other nights the child will be unable to wake up enough to perform. Either way the child's bed may still be wet in the morning. This approach rarely trains the child to learn to get himself up. Usually the child is too sleepy to learn a new routine.

The most useful thing you can do is develop a plan to manage the problem because, for many children, the most common remedy is time: Your child's body needs time to mature physically. He also needs reassurance from you that the problem will end. If you suspect your child's bed wetting is a medical problem, then a trip to the pediatrician's office is essential.

If you feel your child is willfully wetting the bed, or if you sense your child is suffering emotionally, it's time to seek professional help.

WETTING ALARMS

Many pediatricians recommend a conditioning alarm system for older children (ages 7-12) who wet the bed. A buzzer attaches to the child's pajama top with velcro and is connected via a wire to a patch attached to his underpants or pajama bottoms. A drop of moisture on the patch sets the alarm off.

When it goes off, the child is supposed to disconnect the wire to stop the buzzing and run to the bathroom to finish urinating in the toilet. Eventually the alarm should alert the child to listen to the signals from his bladder about the need to pee. For many children the alarm contributes to nighttime control; other children sleep right through the buzzer or disconnect the gadget from their pajamas and continue sleeping.

Parents are often eager to try this mechanical device, but its success is directly related to how highly motivated the child is to succeed. Especially at first, the child needs help from Mom or Dad to manage getting up in the middle of the night and going in the toilet. When the parents and the child follow the product's directions precisely, the success rate is 85%.

Stories from the Bathroom

🦶 Jim was determined to help his son, Martin, overcome bed wetting by using the buzzer alarm. When the buzzer sounded, Jim got up, escorted Martin to the bathroom, made sure he was awake, and had him pee in the toilet. If Martin had already peed his pajamas, Jim woke him up anyway. He wanted Martin to be aware of the fact that he had just peed in his bed. Sometimes he was so deep in sleep Jim splashed water on his face to wake him up.

When Jim and Martin first started this program, they were up five times a night. Jim didn't yell or act exasperated; he just proceeded with extreme patience and discipline. His determination and discipline were eventually adopted by his son. After two months, Martin acquired enough control to sleep through the night without wetting his bed. Sometimes Martin got up during the night to pee, other nights he slept through the night, holding in his urine until he woke up.

Not everyone can muster up the kind of discipline it takes to help a child re-train his sleep patterns. Some parents become too sleep-deprived to remain calm in the middle of the night. If this is true for you, choose one of the other methods of managing bed wetting (such as teaching your child to handle his own laundry) and wait for his body to mature.

Stories from the Bathroom

🦶 Jerry and Brian were best buddies in fifth grade. Jerry invited Brian to spend the night. When Gail, Brian's mom, brought him over to spend the night, the boys ran upstairs to play. Gail introduced herself to Jerry's mom and said, "Brian occasionally has an accident in the middle of the night. He has his sleeping bag and he can sleep on the floor. If he wets, he knows to roll up his pajamas and sleeping bag in the morning and put them in the storage bag. If it's not a problem for you, it's not a problem for Brian." Jane's reply was, "It's not a problem for me."

The next morning no one knew or asked if Brian wet his sleeping bag. He simply managed the situation himself; his self-esteem and his friendship with Jerry remained intact.

SELF-ESTEEM

There is a social expectation that children beyond the age of six years should not wet the bed. There are other developmental expectations we hold for children by six: they should be reading, swimming, and riding a bicycle. The truth is, children vary significantly as to when they achieve these milestones. Nighttime dryness is no different. Children's self-esteem suffers when parents and the rest of society hold onto rigid expectations regarding a child's natural developmental timeline.

Stories from the Bathroom

➤ Tom wet his bed when he was a kid and suffered lots of teasing from friends and siblings. His mom and dad shamed and humiliated him. Tom's son Matthew was now wetting the bed. Painful childhood memories awakened in Tom. He was determined not to let Matthew suffer the embarrassment he experienced as a child.

Tom told Matthew this, "I understand what you're going through. I know how hard it is to be the only one at a sleep-over with a wet sleeping bag." Tom even shared his childhood memories, offering lots of understanding and support to Matthew. He finished with the comment, "If those kids tease you about wetting the bed, then they're not really your friends."

With Tom as Matthew's most important ally, he had enough strength to understand and accept his bed wetting situation. He even developed enough confidence to explain it to others. By age twelve he matured enough physically to remain dry through the night, but most importantly, his self-esteem was secure.

If your child is past six and wets the bed nightly, here are some do's and don'ts to preserve your child's self-esteem.

Do's

- Do explain to your child that bodies develop at different rates in their ability to remain dry all night long, and for him it's just taking longer.
- Do reassure your child that in time he will gain nighttime control.
- Do try a star chart incentive program, but if it isn't effective, drop the plan.
- Do develop a plan for easy laundering of sheets and pajamas that your child can manage mostly on his own.
- Do empathize with your child, "I know you don't want to wet your bed—you don't like wet sheets and pajamas. Someday you'll gain control."

Don'ts

- Don't ask your child each morning if he wet his bed.
- Don't let bed wetting dominate your morning conversation or your relationship between you and your child.
- Don't act disgusted or disappointed if you find a wet bed.
- Don't expect your child to be emotionally distraught over a wet bed.

- Don't discourage your child from spending the night with friends because of this problem.
- Don't allow siblings to tease your child who wets the bed.
- Don't label your child a bed-wetter.
- Don't humiliate, shame or punish your child for wetting the bed.
- Don't compare your child who wets the bed to other children, "Your three-year-old-sister doesn't wet the bed, why do you?"
- Don't constantly talk or call too much attention to the problem. Bed wetting should not dominate the relationship between you and your child.

8

CONSTIPATION, BOWEL RETENTION AND ENCOPRESIS

Before you start teaching your child to have bowel movements in the toilet, notice how often he or she has a bowel movement. Some children go twice a day, others go every other day. It's important to be aware if your child has a natural tendency toward constipation.

Parents whose children constipate easily most likely learn to watch their diets carefully. They also notice if a disruption in their child's schedule triggers constipation, for instance, travel, a simple change in the daily routine (such as going from two naps to one) or a more significant event like starting child care. For some children, just teaching them to poop in the toilet causes constipation.

If this is the case with your child, proceed with caution. It is important as your child learns to have bowel movements in his potty chair that he or she maintain the same bowel regularity. Children who naturally have a tendency toward constipation are often the first to begin to retain their stool around the process of bowel training. Such bowel retention may be a signal your child is resistant to using the toilet.

Bowel retention often occurs when a child is urine trained but requests a diaper for bowel movements. The well-meaning parent wants the child to poop in the toilet, not in the diaper, and refuses to grant the child's request. The child can't bring himself to poop in the toilet, and so keeps the poop in for days. If this is the case with your child, your best option is to give the child a diaper, but develop a practice Poo-Poo Time where the child is required to practice pooping in the toilet, but not expected to perform (see Step Eight, page 75).

Stories from the Bathroom

This is how Melissa proceeded with Elizabeth. Between two-and-a-half and three years old, Elizabeth urine trained quickly. But when she needed to poop, she said, "I need a diaper, Mom." With her diaper in place, off she went to her bedroom for her bowel movement.

Melissa tired of this routine quickly and soon refused to give her a diaper, "No, Elizabeth, you need to poop in the toilet, not in a diaper. You're a big girl now. You pee in the toilet, and you need to poop there too."

Elizabeth sat on the toilet for the longest time but she just couldn't push out a poop. Three days went by with no success. Melissa worried about her daughter's physical well-being from retaining her bowels, so she finally agreed to put a diaper back on for bowel movements.

Melissa consulted the nurse practitioner at her doctor's office. The nurse reassured Melissa that putting the diaper on Elizabeth was the best approach, but also suggested two five-minute practice sessions on the toilet each day. Elizabeth was required to sit on the toilet—she could look at books or listen to music while she sat, but she had to practice. Taking time for these sessions helped Elizabeth adjust to the toilet and within two weeks she was pooping there.

In addition to the practice sessions, Dad and Elizabeth made brown play dough. Melissa purchased a play dough maker at the toy store—a contraption which seems to emulate a bowel movement. This play activity helped Elizabeth understand the pooping process which in turn helped her to eventually overcome her reluctance to have a bowel movement in the toilet.

Although this example occurred with a girl, it is with boys that bowel retention occurs most frequently.

Stories from the Bathroom

One day three-year-old Harrison was on the toilet having a bowel movement. When he flushed, the toilet overflowed.

The erupting toilet and mess terrified him. Mom started to yell, "Get a plunger and a mop! Did you throw something down the toilet? How did this happen?" Mom's understandable reaction increased Harrison's overall anxiety.

After this traumatic experience Harrison refused to poop in the toilet. He began to retain his bowels for three or four days at a time. It wasn't a conscious response on his part, he just never wanted the episode to repeat itself. Delaying bowel movements to gain control over the situation was his unconscious solution.

Mom and Dad worried, but reasonably concluded it was most important for Harrison to resume his regular bowel movements. So they suggested he use a diaper temporarily when he needed to poop. This was just fine with Harrison.

Mom and Dad then encouraged their son to flush the toilet for them. Also, they put Harrison's Teddy bear on the toilet several times a day for a pretend bowel movement. His fear of the toilet slowly disappeared. Within a month, he was back to using the toilet.

ENCOPRESIS*

Constipation and bowel retention are such embarrassing subjects that people are often reluctant to bring the problem up to friends, family, parent educators, nurse practitioners, or even their family physician. If your child becomes occasionally constipated, or starts a steady pattern of retaining his stool beyond four days, it is important to seek help from a doctor who is understanding and knowledgeable on the subject.

If your doctor says, "Don't worry" but you know something is not right with your child's body due to bowel retention, talk to another doctor who listens and offers ideas for help.

A child may refuse to poop in the toilet for many reasons:

- He may have an inherited tendency for constipation.
- The child's family's life may be so hurried there simply isn't time to sit on the toilet. A child might not like to poop in shopping mall toilets, or at day care or school where there are no doors to the toilet stalls, and so will delay having a bowel movement as long as possible.
- Parents may be too severe in their general approach to guiding their child's behavior. A child who feels overly controlled and dominated by his parents sometimes responds to this control by retaining his bowels. Because the parents attempt to control the child's every

---

*For further reading on bowel retention and encopresis, see *Your Child's Health* by B.D. Schmitt, M.D., Bantam Books, New York, 1992.

move, it becomes extremely important to the child that he, and he alone, controls his bowel movements. Bowel retention can result.

- A parent may be too controlling specifically in the area of toilet training and the child is determined that only she will control this bodily function and refuse to perform for Mom or Dad.

- Parents may be too fastidious about cleanliness and unknowingly convey their disgust with the whole natural process of elimination to the child. The result is a child who would rather not poop, wipe, flush, and wash hands and so retains the bowels to avoid all that trouble.

The biggest problem with bowel retention is this: It just keeps getting worse and worse. When the child finally does go, it hurts. So the child delays using the toilet longer. The stool gets bigger, the rectum becomes weak and stretched out, and it hurts more the next time. The child avoids the toilet even more and the situation worsens.

Too often parents go overboard trying to convince their child of the importance of pooping in the toilet on a regular basis. Although talking to your child about the importance of going regularly is sound advice, too much talk is rarely effective when it comes to changing a child's behavior.

If your child waits between six and nine days to go, you must seek medical help because another more complicated and long-term problem can occur: encopresis (commonly referred to as "soiling").

Encopresis occurs when children retain their bowel movements and the stool becomes hard and impacted. Loose stool leaks around the impacted bowel several times a day into the child's underpants, resulting in soiling.

At this point the impacted bowel causes nerve damage to the area, so the child can't feel what's happening and has absolutely no control over the soiling. When soiling continues day after day, the child even becomes accustomed to the smell.

RESPONDING TO SOILING ACCIDENTS

It is important to respond to soiling accidents gently. Your child may not even realize he has leaked diarrhea into his underwear. Don't ignore the soiling, but don't scold the child either. If you smell diarrhea in your child's underpants, either clean him up or have him clean himself up. Keep in mind, you want your child to take as much responsibility as possible for toileting; this includes cleaning himself up and changing his clothes after a soiling incident.

A soiling accident signals the bowel is full. Sit your child on the toilet so he can attempt to empty it. Remember to stay calm and nonchalant. This attempt to poop in the toilet should not seem like a punishment. It's important not to punish or humiliate the child for something he has no control over.

Do not allow siblings and friends to tease a child with a soiling problem. Stop the teasers immediately and explain the situation to encourage empathy rather than shame. Here's all you need to say, "Jason leaked diarrhea into his underpants, he can't help it. I will not allow you to tease him. Come on Jason, let's change your clothes."

Children suffering with encopresis need help. Because soiling is embarrassing and emotionally charged, parents are often reluctant to mention it to their doctors. But if your child retains bowel movements for more than a week, and has bouts of diarrhea, talk to your physician without delay.

Children or teens who suffer from encopresis can do damage to their colons and may require surgeries later as adults to repair the damage. Encopresis can harm a child's body as well as his self-esteem. Bowel retention is not something you can just ignore and hope will go away.

WHAT TO DO

When a child has an impacted bowel, the first step is to clear it. Some doctors recommend enemas to clear the impaction. Other doctors treat the child with oral medication to loosen and eventually free the impacted bowel. It is important not to give enemas, suppositories, or laxatives without consulting your doctor.

Once the impacted bowel is cleared, some doctors suggest oral stool softeners and a high fiber diet to keep the child from becoming constipated again. Stool softeners make the stool soft and easy to pass.

Mineral oil is another remedy commonly used today. It helps stool to slip out of the child's body easily. If your doctor recommends mineral oil, keep it in the refrigerator; it tastes better cold. Children can take it with fruit juice, or mixed with a cola drink. For most children, mineral oil depletes the body's natural vitamins, so ask your doctor if your child needs a vitamin supplement each day.

Follow your doctor's recommendation regarding the right amount of mineral oil for your child. If he is getting too much you will begin to see oil spots on his underwear. If he starts to get constipated again, he's probably not getting enough.

Mineral oil and other stool softeners are not laxatives; they do not cause contractions or pressure. They simply lubricate the bowel so the stool can slip out, thus avoiding the recurring incidence of an impacted bowel.

Once your child's bowel has been cleaned out and he starts taking mineral oil (or another stool softener) and eating a non-constipating diet, ask your doctor how long you'll need to continue this course of action. For some children it's three months, for others, up to a year. It takes time for the bowel muscles to re-strengthen and manage pushing out the stool without lubrication.

HOW DIET CAN HELP

If your child has a natural tendency toward constipation, it's important to provide a non-constipating diet.

However, if your child's bowel is already impacted, don't push the healthy foods quite yet. The impaction needs clearing first. Offer liquids and follow your doctor's instructions on loosening the impaction and getting it passed.

After the bowel is cleared, your child needs raw fruits and vegetables every day. Bran, with its high fiber content, is an excellent natural laxative. Some breads and cereals contain bran. Milk products and cooked carrots contribute to constipation, so limit these.

PRACTICE SESSIONS

Children who have had an impacted bowel for a long time often lose the natural urge to defecate due to nerve damage. Practice sessions provide an opportunity for the child who isn't feeling the urge-to-go signal to pass stool into the toilet. Set aside two Poo-Poo Times each day (even if he doesn't feel the need to go) during which he is required to sit on the toilet for ten minutes to practice, or until a bowel movement is passed, whichever comes first. The best time for results is often about 25 minutes after a meal.

As your child sits on the toilet, encourage him to push, grunt, and bear down. Demonstrate this action to your child if necessary. The child needs to understand a bowel movement doesn't just drop out—it takes some effort. Tell your child to bend forward so that his chest touches his upper legs while he sits on the toilet. It also helps to have a short stool for your child to rest his feet on. This provides pushing leverage.

At first, accompany your child for these sessions on the toilet. Read or tell your child a story. You want this time to be relaxed, rather than a source of tension. Play some music, give the child a toy to manipulate as he sits, and then demonstrate and encourage actions to push a poop out. Keep this time positive and upbeat. It is important to find a time for toilet sitting that is convenient for you, because your child needs your positive involvement and attention. Don't start this potty-sitting time as an afterthought as you're rushing out the door in the morning.

If your child attends child care or school, it's important to incorporate the teachers' assistance. They need to allow your child to go to the bathroom *whenever* the urge strikes, without waiting for permission. Be sure to keep a change of clothes at school.

One family whose child was retaining his bowel movements, sometimes up to nine days, received help from an Encopresis Clinic at their local children's hospital. After the impacted bowel was cleared, the clinic suggested daily doses of mineral oil, plus a toileting schedule: The child was to sit on the toilet for 15 minutes, twice a day. He wasn't forced to poop in the toilet, he was just encouraged to try. It took a year before he was on a normal pooping routine without the mineral oil or scheduled toilet sitting times. Patience and a matter-of-fact approach from his parents were key to ending the bowel retention.

PREVENTING ENCOPRESIS

If you're in the process of toilet training your toddler, you want to do all you can to prevent bowel retention and encopresis. But keep in mind the biggest contributing factor to these problems is an inherited tendency for constipation. So if you know your child has a problem with constipation, here are some tips to prevent bowel retention and encopresis:

- Don't start toilet training too soon. Wait until the child is ready. Before you launch into bowel training, re-read the readiness signs listed at the end of Chapter 1.

- Remember children today are trained somewhere between two and three years old—girls often before boys. Further, children usually learn to be bowel trained and urine trained separately. These are two totally different processes to learn to control. So work on one at a time.

- Don't get into a power struggle over toileting. An emotional battle can result in your child refusing to use the toilet and retaining his bowels. Remember, ultimate control lies with the child. It's his body; he's the one in charge. You can encourage, reward, influence, and motivate, but you can't force a child to poop. If toileting has become emotionally charged, back off, give it a month or two, and then try again.

- Understand that all people don't have a bowel movement every day. Some people go two or three times a day and some go every three days. Both are normal. But if your child usually goes twice a day in a diaper and now because of bowel training is only going every other day, consider that a warning sign. Consult your pediatrician if you are unsure of what is normal for children.

- When you're changing your child's diapers, don't act repulsed or disgusted with the natural process of elimination. Be glad your child is eliminating. And if your child has an accident, don't say, "How can you stand that icky poop in your pants? It's dirty and disgusting." Just nonchalantly clean the child and state, "Oops, you had an accident. It's okay. I know someday you'll poop in the toilet."

- If your urine-trained child asks for a diaper when it's time for a bowel movement, go ahead and put one on. He needs to be in control of when and where he has his bowel movement. If the parent refuses to provide the diaper, the child might refuse to poop, starting the negative cycle of bowel retention and encopresis. Even though the child is urine trained, he just isn't ready to poop in the toilet. Physically and intellectually the child is ready, but emotionally he isn't ready to give up those diapers.

- When your child is learning to use the toilet, provide lots of opportunities to play with dirt, mud, sand, and play dough. Purchase a play dough press at the toy store. This tactile play is therapeutic; children can come to terms with the process of elimination through this messy play experience.

- Encourage a healthy diet. Offer your child lots of fruits, vegetables, and whole grain foods.

If bowel training results in power struggles and encopresis, make an appointment to see your doctor and possibly a psychologist specializing in children and play therapy.

ONE FINAL TIP

It is important to give children reasonable control through choices (appropriate to the child's developmental age and ability, of course). Children can make choices about clothing, food, friends, and toys. If children have *some* positive control in their life, controlling their bowel movements won't become so critical to them.

Stories from the Bathroom

👣 When Ryan turned 18 months old, his mom, Colleen, placed a little potty chair in the bathroom. This was the same time frame she had used with Ryan's older sister, who quickly learned to use the toilet just after her second birthday. Colleen's success with her first child gave her experience and confidence.

Colleen was doing nothing more than acquainting Ryan with the potty chair. She knew he was too young to train, she just wanted to familiarize him with the process. At first Ryan liked the potty chair. He'd sit there and chat with his sister as she took a bath. Then, inexplicably, Ryan began to dislike the potty chair and even avoid the bathroom.

At his age, Ryan was not a child easily coaxed into doing anything—from getting into a car seat to going to bed at a reasonable time each night. So it wasn't too surprising when he started showing signs of resisting toileting.

Ryan was also fussy about being clean. He wouldn't play in sand or dirt and frequently washed his hands. He was a logical candidate to avoid the whole messy process of pooping into the toilet.

As Ryan approached his second birthday, he started holding in his bowel movements. The most drastic stretch of time was ten days. That's when Colleen called the doctor, who prescribed a baby laxative. The miserable feeling in Ryan's system before taking the laxative, and the feeling as the laxative went to work, reinforced Ryan's negative association with the whole process of elimination.

After only three or four days of no bowel movements, Colleen, upon the advice of her doctor, offered Milk of Magnesia® to end the constipation and clean out his system. Eventually she noticed Ryan's body never seemed to manage a bowel movement without the Milk of Magnesia.®

She called her doctor again and was referred to a pediatric gastroenterologist who advised her to give him one tablespoon of mineral oil each day. She tried giving it to him mixed with chocolate milk. He refused to drink it. Then she tried mixing it with peanut butter and spreading it on bread. He could tell the peanut butter was different and refused to eat the sandwich. Finally, in desperation, she mixed the oil with a little cola in a tiny cup. Ryan had never tasted soda pop before and drank it down without hesitation.

The mineral oil eased the process of eliminating stools. There was no more pain when Ryan tried to poop and there were no more stomachaches accompanied by bowel retention. Slowly he lost his fear and disgust of the pooping process. By age three he started going in the toilet.

The doctor warned that he might need to take the mineral oil for a long time. His body lacked the natural lubricant required for bowel movements. Ryan's dad had a similar problem as a child, for which he was hospitalized. So hereditary factors also played a significant part in Ryan's tendency toward constipation and bowel retention.

One mom made this statement regarding her daughter's problem with bowel retention and soiling, "I never thought my days would revolve around my child's pooping schedule. We were forced to slow our days down as she learned to poop regularly on the toilet during her practice sessions. It took a year until she was pooping on a regular schedule. As I look back, I don't know how we managed, but we did. I'm so relieved it's over."

This mom had to temporarily set her daily tasks aside to assist her daughter in changing her bowel habits. If your child has a similar problem, you may be facing this too; you will need medical advice and a plan which includes mustering up lots of patience for the sake of your child.

CHECKLIST FOR DEALING WITH
BOWEL RETENTION & ENCOPRESIS

☑ Adopt a gentle and supportive attitude.

☑ Consult your child's doctor and follow her advice on clearing the impacted bowel.

☑ Adjust your child's diet.

☑ Administer stool softeners as your doctor recommends.

☑ Establish two practice sessions on the toilet each day.

☑ Enlist the support and cooperation of your child's teacher or caregiver.

9

PUTTING IT ALL TOGETHER

A mom asked this question: "What if you did nothing when it comes to toilet training? Would your child eventually learn to pee and poop in the toilet on his own?"

It's just about impossible for a parent to do nothing. Simply because parents use the toilet themselves, children get the message they are expected to eventually learn to use the toilet too. Many children ease into training with little more than a few suggestions from Mom or Dad and some practice. Then, when their bowel and bladder muscles develop and strengthen, they learn to use the toilet without much fuss. Toilet training with ease is the hope of all parents for their children.

Just as children eventually learn behaviors like sitting at the table to eat three meals a day, sleeping through the night, and skills such as reading, bike riding, and much later driving a car, most children between two and three years old learn to use the toilet. It's a training process that requires your guidance, positive attention, and interest. Of course, you must model the desired behavior and be your child's mentor in training. Also, you might need to develop a couple of rules to provide some clear discipline as you guide your child toward using the toilet.

Your general approach toward discipline will certainly impact how toilet training progresses with your child.

PARENTING STYLES

Each parent has an approach to parenting that is evident in how they train their child to do anything from sleeping through the night—to toilet training—to helping children complete their homework. In parenting there are three distinct styles; notice the category where you fit.

The Take-Charge Parent

Some parents have a take-charge approach. They supervise children closely and are strict and clear about their expectations. This does not mean they are unloving or cold, it just means that when it's time to teach a child to use the toilet, they don't hedge. They are decisive. They develop a plan and proceed with confidence.

The Diplomatic Parent

Other parents take a diplomatic approach to discipline. They have goals when it comes to guiding their children, but they make a conscious attempt to be sensitive to the needs of their children, whether they are teaching them to use the toilet or ride a bicycle. They are usually willing to compromise and negotiate. They alter their expectations according to each child's temperament and development. They keep their parenting goals clear, but continually observe their children's progress and respond in the best interest of each child.

The Laissez-Faire Parent

The laissez-faire approach is the third style. Parents in this category are less intrusive when it comes to guiding their children. They don't make too many demands. They trust that in time children—mostly on their own—will learn manners, tidiness, and toileting. Discipline is low-key and unimposing. Many parents who take this laid-back approach are uninvolved. Others are very involved, but believe a gentle, accepting, and non-intrusive style fosters the most secure, loved, and accomplished child.

Which category do you fall into? When it comes to toilet training, each discipline style will work with some children and not with others. However, parents who embrace the diplomatic style are usually most successful when it comes to toilet training. The take-charge parent, for example, might need to back off. A parent with a laissez-faire style might need to set a limit around toilet training. And even the diplomatic parent can go awry; this parent can come across as wishy-washy to the child. The diplomatic parent sometimes tries too hard to be in tune with the child and changes her approach to toilet training frequently, hoping to find the method best suited to the child.

The following stories show how each style has its pitfalls.

Stories from the Bathroom

David wanted two-and-a-half-year-old Patrick trained. He was clear and determined. He put Patrick in underpants and told him to keep his pants dry and clean. He made it clear that Patrick was expected to pee and poop in the toilet.

Patrick balked. He had accident after accident and refused to perform on the toilet. He wet or pooped his pants right after sitting on his toilet seat. After a week of no success, David realized that he must alter his tactics. He put Patrick back in diapers. He set him on the toilet twice a day to practice and then started using underpants part-time until Patrick gained control. Slowly, Patrick became willing to use the toilet.

Patrick made it perfectly clear he needed a more gradual approach when it came to learning to use the toilet. He just couldn't succeed with his dad's method. Even though it wasn't David's parenting style to back off, he did. He didn't give up, he simply provided a more flexible, alternate plan. In this way, David helped Patrick gradually take charge of his own bodily functions.

𝕀 Marie asked Daniel each day if he wanted to wear diapers or underwear. She wanted Daniel to choose; she believed that he and he alone needed to be in charge. But the daily decision to wear diapers or underpants went on way too long. About three days a week Daniel chose diapers, the other days he chose underpants.

Finally it appeared that Daniel had control of his bowels and bladder, but on the days he wore diapers, he didn't bother with using the toilet. The daily routine of choosing underpants or diapers was hindering complete toilet training success. Marie hated to do it, but finally she declared, "No more diapers."

Daniel pouted, complained, and cried, but Mom remained firm in her stand. She was uncomfortable with Daniel's emotional response and wanted to spare him discomfort, but both she and Daniel endured the tears. In three days Daniel gave up asking for diapers and used the toilet consistently.

🦶 Nancy was low-key in her approach to parenting—including toilet training. Then this scenario began to occur: Her three-year-old daughter had an accident almost every time they went for a ride in the car. Nancy hoped Jennifer would learn on her own to pee before getting in the car, but her daughter continued to have accident after accident. Finally, Nancy lost her patience.

Although it was contrary to her parenting style, Nancy imposed a rule: Jennifer must try to pee in the toilet before any car ride. Of course, Nancy couldn't force Jennifer to perform on the toilet, but most often Jennifer would go. Nancy needed to change her laid-back approach so Jennifer could be spared the embarrassment and hassle of wet clothes on every outing in the car.

COMBINING DIFFERENT PARENTING STYLES

When more than one person is involved in guiding a child to use the toilet, conflict can arise if one has a completely different style than the other. If two parents argue or proceed with two completely different methods, the child becomes confused. Whose rules should he follow? Parents need to compromise, negotiate, and develop *one* plan for toilet training their child. When parents provide consistency, children learn more quickly and easily. Here's how one diplomatic mom and take-charge dad met in the middle for their child's sake.

Stories from the Bathroom

🦶 Sandy started teaching Robert to use the toilet in her usual low-key manner. When Dad came home he took on the task with more force and determination. He set rules: no more diapers and wet pants or TV privileges were taken away. Robert was confused by the difference in styles and did not make much progress. Finally the couple sought counseling.

This is how they resolved the conflict. Because Sandy was the primary caregiver, she would be in charge of teaching Robert to use the toilet. But when Dad came home, he and Robert would use the toilet together, including a practice time on the toilet before bedtime. Dad was able to provide some rules and be Robert's positive role model without confusing Robert about whose approach to follow. Dad's new plan for the evening fit in with Mom's low-key approach during the day. Robert benefited from Dad's involvement and the new consistency of style. He soon made progress.

TIMING IS KEY

When it comes to guiding children toward a new competency, it's important to choose the right time. We don't teach two year olds to read and we don't train three year olds to ride a two-wheel bicycle. Immature and under-developed bodies and minds are not equipped to learn advanced skills, no matter how qualified the instruction. Education must mesh with a child's developing ability to learn a new task. If a child's physical maturation is out of sync with instruction for toilet training, frustration occurs rather than competency.

On the other hand, don't let the opportunity for learning slip by. If a child's body is ready to learn a new skill, teach it; but don't be surprised if she objects. Reluctance is a common response to change. Give the child time to adjust to the new learning experience. Newness causes emotional upheaval; it doesn't mean the child can't learn the skill.

Most seven year olds can learn to swim; most six and a half year olds are ready to learn to read; and most two and a half year olds can begin to learn to use the toilet. If you wait months, or even years longer, children get set in their ways and resist or fear the change learning a new skill brings.

Knowing or sensing when the time is right for your child to learn a new behavior is a key to effective parenting. Physical maturation of the body is often necessary before a child can master a new skill, but it isn't isolated. A child is more complex. Parents must keep in mind the child's intellectual, social, and emotional development and maturity as they train their child to learn the skills required of them in our society.

TWO YEAR OLDS: THE DEMAND FOR AUTONOMY

It's normal and necessary for your two year old to make statements like these: "No! Leave me alone. I do it my way." At the same time toddlers gain control of their bowels and bladder, they push to define themselves as separate from you. The combination of these two factors, true to toddler development, makes toileting instruction more difficult.

Why didn't Mother Nature put toilet training at a more compliant age? Believe it or not, there is a benefit to toilet training and the "Terrible Twos" going hand in hand. You have to learn how to positively direct your child toward the desired goal, all the while respecting her as a separate individual with her own unique temperament and style of learning. This is a valuable parenting skill to attain.

Children control their attitudes and emotional responses to any situation. They and they alone control what their bodies do. Respect from you for this separateness contributes to their self-esteem and personal responsibility.

When you become too enmeshed in your child's feelings, behaviors, and attitudes, problems occur. This is true whether you're encouraging your child to learn to use the toilet or helping her to improve her reading ability. It's important to keep in mind the boundaries of your control and influence.

MAINTAIN A LOVING RELATIONSHIP

The better your relationship is with your child, the more influence you will have in your child's life and the easier it will be to teach him new skills. Never take it for granted that your child knows how much you love him. You must demonstrate it with your words and actions every day. Here are some suggestions.

☑ Tell your child you love him. Do it routinely as you tuck him in bed each night, or spontaneously as you're changing his diaper, or as he sits on the potty chair for the first time. When your child works on a puzzle or when he's older and doing his homework, bestow an "I love you." When your child sits on your lap, whisper, "I'm glad you're my kid." It feels good to your child—and to you too.

☑ Seek opportunities daily to communicate love through gentle touch. When your child tries to poop into the toilet kneel down and gently touch her back or legs. Pull her on your lap to read a story. Cuddle her when she's sad. Massage her back, legs, and arms when her muscles are tired from a tough day at play. Touch communicates love without saying a word.

☑ Compliment your child. Notice baby steps toward competency. "I saw you sitting on the toilet trying to pee— good for you." "I saw you take your plate from the table to the counter—I really appreciate that." "I was so proud of you today when you thanked Grandma for the cookies. Such nice manners." These compliments not only reinforce positive behavior, but because you took time to notice, you're saying, "I love you."

☑ Guide your child clearly and respectfully toward appropriate behavior. There are ways to discipline that preserve dignity and self-esteem, and there are attempts at discipline that tear down a child's self-image. Some days you'll get it right, some days you won't.

Upholding a rule provides security in a child's world; this equals love. Insisting a child sit on the toilet to try to pee before a car ride provides a reasonable limit, develops a positive routine, and brings security and predictability to a child's life. Reasonable rules—even though they may elicit a little emotional resistance from the child as they're being taught and instilled—are a powerful expression of love. Rules tell your child you care.

☑ Brag to others about your child and let her overhear. Call Dad at work with this news, "Jayme sat on the toilet and peed twice today." If someone else compliments your child to you, repeat it to your child. Some parents worry in an old-fashioned sense that praise will produce conceited children. Certainly we don't want little princes and princesses running around believing every little thing they do is just darling, but we do want children who are quietly self-assured. So go ahead and do some bragging and let your child hear it.

☑ Observe your child. As your son puts his doll on and off the toilet in play, stop to observe. When your daughter is drawing a picture of an airplane, ask if you can watch. As she practices the piano, sit down and listen. This sounds simple, but it's an easy and powerful way to express a silent "I love you."

☑ Help them out. If Benjamin is struggling to get his pants up after peeing in the toilet, leave your phone conversation to help. If Lily is struggling to find her backpack, lunch box, or coat as she's running out the door for the school bus, help her out. If your children want to build a fort, but are frustrated gathering the materials and developing the plans, step in and help. Don't take over and don't do it for them—just help.

☑ Participate in your child's interests and hobbies. When he takes an interest in the toilet, support that interest. Let him flush the toilet for you or give you toilet paper. When your children are older, go to their dance recitals, school performances, and soccer games. Hunt through baseball card shops for that special sought-after card. Children's interests are important. When you support their interests, you're telling them they are important to you. Showing interest strengthens the parent-child relationship.

☑ Learn the technique referred to as "completing the cycle of the conversation." When your toddler says, "My Teddy pooped his pants," don't ignore your child. Instead say, "You better change him. I bet he'll learn to poop in the toilet someday."

When your child, now eight years old, says, "My friend Mary is moving to Chicago" don't just say, "Oh" or "Don't worry, you'll find another friend." Instead respond this way, "When is she moving?" and "I bet you'll miss her." Your reply communicates, "I heard what you said, I'm interested, and I want to hear more."

☑ Cheer your child on. As your child begins to use the toilet, quietly cheer each success. Any effort toward competency deserves your applause. Whether it's reading, basketball, or working on a model airplane, offer encouragement. And when she experiences failure, be there to wipe her tears. Help her learn from her mistakes and to try another approach.

All parents love their children, but it takes skill to demonstrate this love. When you and your child are connected by a relationship based in love, it will be easier for you to teach your child to use the toilet and many other necessary skills.

FINAL TIPS & REMINDERS

Some parents need just a little information when it comes to teaching their children to use the toilet. They have good instincts about how to ease their children naturally into toilet training. Other parents need all the ideas available. For all of you, here are some final tips to help the process along.

Avoid Friction

Steer away from emotional friction and tension when it comes to guiding your child to use the toilet. If you sense yourself growing more and more emotional and out of control, back off, assess the situation, and call someone for help and ideas—your doctor, a nurse, your mother, a friend, or a parent educator.

Put the Process Into Words

As you coach your child toward using the toilet, gently and calmly put the process into words. Simple explanations regarding what is happening right now and what will happen next help children go from an emotional response to an intellectual understanding. Don't go overboard trying to convince your child that the plan is a good one, expecting agreement. Just explain what toilet training is about. Offer only small doses of explanation each step of the way.

Work With Your Child

Work with—not against—your two year old. This is easy advice to give, but often difficult to carry out. Independence and non-compliance are normal and important parts of being two years old. Skillfully, you must make your two year old believe that using the toilet is his idea. Use positive influence and resist pressure tactics. If you sense yourself getting exasperated, tense, or angry, back off. Readjust your frame of mind. Don't engage in a power struggle; you'll lose. Pressure won't work.

Be Realistic

Don't let one success lure you into believing your child is now completely trained. You'll hear parents claim their child was trained in one day. This may be true for a few children, but most learn to use the toilet gradually over about one month's time. Build on your child's successes, but don't believe that one poop in the toilet will lead to complete training. Rather, recognize each successful step as part of the process.

Take Along a Favorite Toy

Let your toddler take whatever he wants with him to the toilet. Toddlers love to tote toys around the house. The trip to the bathroom just comes easier if your toddler takes a favorite toy along for company. The psychology works this way: You get your child to sit on the potty and your child gets to choose a toy or book for company. Both of you get something out of the visit to the bathroom.

Switch to Cloth Diapers for Training

If you use disposable diapers, consider using cloth diapers as your child approaches the age of toilet training. Cloth diapers help a child learn the difference between wet and dry. This is what you want. There are disposable training diapers on the market that claim children will feel the sensation of wetness. You might want to try these. Also, change your child frequently and say, "I'm changing your diaper because it's wet (or messy)." Say this as a point of information—never with a hint of disapproval. Your child will begin to differentiate between wet and dry and messy and clean.

Keep it Positive

Toilet training goes easily for many parents and children. But some children resist the whole process. Remember this: Toilet training is important, but it's more important that your child develops positive associations with the toileting process. If you yell, spank, coerce, or manipulate your child to use the toilet, your child may grow to resist and resent one of the most common and natural functions in daily life. That's why your positive and pleasant frame of mind is so important.

Treat Your Child with Dignity

Toileting involves the most private part of a child's body. This personal area deserves your respect. For this reason, it's important to do your best to preserve your child's dignity—whether you're assisting with wiping or respecting your child's request for privacy. Keep the importance of respect in mind as you work toward the desired goal of total toileting independence.

Children are accustomed to using diapers. Your job is to cultivate an interest in using the toilet. Be careful that toileting doesn't become more important to you than it is to your child. She needs your attention, guidance, and support to make this transition from diapers to underpants. When your child is toilet trained, she will have reached an important developmental milestone.

When training is complete, look back and reflect. How did you go about the process? What techniques helped you succeed? Which steps were ineffective? It will be interesting to notice if your child masters other developmental milestones—reading, bike riding, swimming—in much the same manner. What did you learn about your child as you guided her toward toileting success? What did you learn about yourself as a parent? Your own stories from the bathroom will be a testament of growth and learning for you and your child. Do your parenting best to make the toilet training journey positive for both you and your child.

Average Children's Toilet Training Progress by Months*

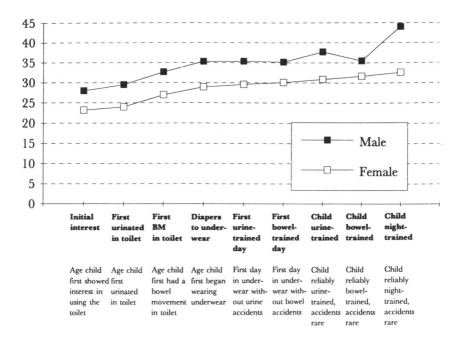

	Initial interest	First urinated in toilet	First BM in toilet	Diapers to under- wear	First urine- trained day	First bowel- trained day	Child urine- trained	Child bowel- trained	Child night- trained
	Age child first showed first interest in using the toilet	Age child first urinated in toilet	Age child first had a bowel movement in toilet	Age child first began wearing underwear	First day in under- wear with- out urine accidents	First day in under- wear with- out bowel accidents	Child reliably urine- trained, accidents rare	Child reliably bowel- trained, accidents rare	Child reliably night- trained, accidents rare

*Data from a study of Washington State families, conducted by Jan Faull, 1995.

This data was collected by the author in a study of approximately 100 children. The ages shown are the average times boys and girls from this group reached each milestone. (For children who experienced regression, it occured between the ages of 31 to 35 months. The regression lasted, on average, about one month.)

Books for Parents to Read to Their Children

Blau, Judith H. *Stop and Go Potty!* Taipei, Taiwan: Random House, 1993. A cloth book with an attached doll that moves from page to page as you read the book. The book shows a child involved in lots of activities "but sometimes I have to stop and go potty."

Borgardt, Marianne. *What Do You Do With a Potty*, New York: Western Publishing Co., Inc., 1994. How and why to use a potty chair in an appealing pop-up format.

Brooks, Joae Graham, M.D. *No More Diapers!* New York: Dell Publishing, 1971. There are three sections to this book: one for parents, one for boys, one for girls. Two stories tell of a boy and then a girl going from diapers to learning to urinate and have bowel movements in a potty chair. The approach offers information and a dose of common sense.

Cole, Joanna. *Your New Potty*, New York: Mulberry Books, 1989. A straightforward story line provides children with a clear idea of how girls and boys go from diapers to using the potty chair. Photographs.

Frankel, Alona. *Once Upon a Potty*, Hauppauge, New York: Barron's Educational Series, Inc., 1979. A story about a child who goes from peeing and pooping in diapers to using the potty. This book shows the child's body parts and illustrates bowel movements and urinating. There is a version for boys and one for girls.

Galvin, Matthew. *Clouds and Clocks*, New York: Magination Press, 1989. Too long and complicated for preschoolers, but appropriate for school-aged children who soil their underpants. An important book.

Gomi, Taro. *Everyone Poops*, Brooklyn, New York: Kane/Miller Publishers, 1993. Children are interested in most natural phenomenons, including bowel movements. This books tells about animal poop and its different shapes, colors, and smells. The book concludes with, "All living things eat, so everyone poops."

Holzwarth, Werner and Erlbruch, Wolf. *The Story of the Little Mole Who Went in Search of Whodunit*, New York: Stewart, Tabori & Chang, 1993. Children enjoy this fun story about a Mole who got pooped on and his search for the culprit "whodunit."

Langley, Jonathan, and Civardi, Anne. *Potty Time*, New York: Simon & Schuster, 1988. Sweet pictures illustrate this story which chronicles the major steps in going from diapers to underpants, and then going from a potty chair to the big toilet. The book uses the terms "Number One" and "Number Two" for urinating and bowel movements.

Lansky, Vicki. *KoKo Bear's New Potty*, New York: Bantam Books, 1988. KoKo Bear gets a potty, underpants, has accidents, and is finally successful. On each page there are tips and information for parents.

Lewison, Wendy Cheyette. *The Princess and the Potty*, New York: Simon & Schuster, 1994. An appealing story for children with a fairy tale quality about a princess who refuses to use the potty. When she wishes to wear pantalettes like the queen, she becomes motivated.

Mills, Joyce and Crowley, Richard. *Sammy the Elephant and Mr. Camel: A Story to Help Children Overcome Bedwetting While Discovering Self-Appreciation*, New York: Magination Press, 1988. Sammy the elephant gradually learns to control his body as he grows and develops. If your child wets the bed, this book will help him understand the situation while building self-esteem.

Munsch, Robert. *I Have To Go!* Toronto, Canada: Annick Press, Ltd., 1992. A cute story about a common dilemma. Mom and Dad ask the child if he needs to use the toilet before climbing in bed, getting in the car, or going outside. He always says, "No!" but soon needs to go.

Rogers, Fred. *Going to the Potty*, New York: G.P. Putnam & Sons, 1986. This book shows children how they change and grow in many ways, including urinating and having bowel movements in diapers and then in the toilet. Photographs of children illustrate the book.

von Konigslow, Andrea Wayne. *Toilet Tales*, Toronto, Canada: Annick Press, Ltd., 1991. This charming, simple story explains why various animals don't sit on the toilet. The story ends with the line, "Toilets are meant for big kids like you."

Books for Parents

Azrin, Nathan and Besalel, Victor. *A Parent's Guide to Bedwetting Control*, New York: Simon & Schuster, 1979. This "take charge" approach to bedwetting control includes encouraging the child to drink as much liquid as possible and waking the child up every hour until midnight or 1:00am to change wet sheets or go to the toilet. Advises parent and child to keep a calendar of dry and wet nights.

Azrin, Nathan and Foxx, Richard. *Toilet Training in Less Than a Day*, New York: Simon & Schuster, 1974. Parents are instructed to push liquids and salty foods during toilet training. Children are encouraged to practice running to the bathroom from different places in the house. The program is intense and may produce temper tantrums and resistance to toilet training.

Brazelton, T. Barry. *Toddlers & Parents*, New York: A Delta Book, 1974. Offers parents a clear idea of what it's like to toilet train a toddler. The story of a little boy explains the trials and triumphs he experiences as he reaches this developmental milestone. Information about the inner developmental life of the toddler is included.

Cole, Joanna. *Parents™ Book of Toilet Learning*, New York: Ballantine Books, 1983. The author makes a case for the importance of using the terms "teaching" and "learning" rather than "training" when it comes to guiding children to use the toilet. Full of valuable information.

Lansky, Vicki. *Toilet Training*, New York: Bantam Books, 1993. A quick guide to toilet training. Offers a lot of tips from parents: what worked, what didn't. Photographs of various potty chairs and seats.

Leach, Penelope. *Your Baby & Child*, New York: Alfred A. Knopf, 1990. In this information-packed book about baby and child care is a short section on toilet training. The information is sensible and practical.

Mack, Alison. *Dry All Night*, Boston, MA: Little, Brown & Co., 1989. This book has two sections. The first is for parents and the second is for school-age children who wet the bed to read alone. Encourages kids to take complete responsibility for the situation.

Mack, Alison. *Toilet Learning*, Boston, MA: Little, Brown & Co., 1978. The first section is for parents and the second is for parents to read aloud to their children. The author gives a broad perspective of the toileting process and warns parents not to miss the period of peak readiness.

Schaefer, Charles, M.D. *Toilet Training Without Tears*, New York: Signet, 1989. Dr. Schaefer not only offers a plan for toilet training but includes valuable information if a child is frequently constipated, retentive, or has encopresis. If your child is over three and a half and resistant to urine or bowel training, be sure to read this book.

Scharf, Martin. *Waking Up Dry: How to End Bedwetting Forever*, Cincinnati, OH: Writer's Digest Books, 1986. A structured approach for ending bedwetting using a wetness alarm. If you are considering purchasing a wetness alarm, read this book first.

Schmitt, Barton. *Your Child's Health*, New York: Bantam Books, 1991. In this complete guide to children's health issues is a section on toilet training. A list of "Do's" and "Don'ts" to prevent problems is included, as well as a section on children who resist training. Valuable reading if your child is retaining bowel movements or constipated.

Van Pelt, Katie. *Potty Training Your Baby*, Garden City Park, NY: Avery Publishing Group, Inc., 1988. Advises parents to "Start as soon as a baby is able to sit up on his on own and remain sitting for a good while without support." Most parents today don't use this early start, nevertheless, the book is valuable for its good advice regarding a pleasant attitude and frame of mind when it comes to toilet training.

More Books To Help Parents

Go To Your Room: Consequences That Teach helps parents improve the daily behavior of their children by choosing and using logical consequences that will work. Useful with ages 3-14. • $14.95

Without Spanking Or Spoiling combines the best information from four major parenting approaches. It allows parents to choose a guidance method that best fits their child's temperament and their family values. Includes 150 ideas for overcoming common behavior problems. • $14.95

The Sleep Book for Tired Parents is full of help for solving children's sleep problems. This book offers options and practical suggestions to ease children and parents into a sleep pattern the whole family can live with. Discusses three major techniques: Family Bed, Cry-It-Out, and Teach-in-Small-Steps. • $14.95

Tools for Everyday Parenting Series are great books for new parents. They present information in both text and cartoon illustrations. Each practical book offers tried-and-true tools for improving parenting skills. • Titles include: *Peekaboo & Other Games to Play with Your Baby, Joyful Play with Toddlers, Magic Tools for Raising Kids, 365 Wacky, Wonderful Ways to Get Your Children to Do What You Want,* and *Taking Care of Me.* $11.95 each

Feelings for Little Children series are designed to offer young children alternatives. The full-color rhyming board books can be read or sung. • Titles include: *When You're HAPPY and You Know It, When You're MAD and You Know It, When You're SHY and You Know It,* and *When You're SILLY and You Know It.* $5.95 each, or four for $23.80.

Ask for these books at your favorite bookstore, call 1-800-992-6657, or visit us on the Internet at www.Parentingpress.com. Visa/Mastercard accepted. A complete catalog is available upon request.

Parenting Press, Inc., dept. 603, P.O. Box 75267, Seattle, WA 98175. In Canada, please call Raincoast Book Distribution, 1-800-661-5450.